Mythic Creatures

Dracio ad sanctum georgium mart..
au de signū teres
xpi. Qui a scibi
meruit. Multū
collegio Saude
magū conuertasse.
Et puellam eruisse. A dracone ra..

AMERICAN MUSEUM ᴏꜰ NATURAL HISTORY

Mythic Creatures

And the Impossibly Real Animals Who Inspired Them

Adapted from an exhibition curated by
LAUREL KENDALL & MARK A. NORELL
with **RICHARD ELLIS** *and the*
American Museum of Natural History
Exhibition Department

Sterling Signature
NEW YORK

AMERICAN MUSEUM
OF NATURAL HISTORY

Sterling Signature
NEW YORK

An Imprint of Sterling Publishing Co., Inc.
1166 Avenue of the Americas
New York, NY 10036

ISBN 978-1-4549-2219-3

Distributed in Canada by Sterling Publishing Co., Inc.
c/o Canadian Manda Group, 664 Annette Street
Toronto, Ontario, Canada M6S 2C8
Distributed in the United Kingdom by GMC Distribution Services
Castle Place, 166 High Street, Lewes, East Sussex, England BN7 1XU
Distributed in Australia by NewSouth Books
45 Beach Street, Coogee, NSW 2034, Australia

For information about custom editions, special sales, and premium and corporate purchases, please
contact Sterling Special Sales at 800-805-5489 or specialsales@sterlingpublishing.com.

Manufactured in Canada

2 4 6 8 10 9 7 5 3 1

www.sterlingpublishing.com

Design by Ashley Prine, Tandem Books

See picture credits page 192

The **American Museum of Natural History** is one of the world's preeminent scientific, educational, and cultural institutions. Since its founding in 1869, the Museum has pursued its mission—to discover, interpret, and share information about human cultures, the natural world, and the universe—through a broad program of scientific research, education, and exhibition.

Each year, millions of visitors experience the Museum's 45 permanent exhibition halls, which include world-famous diorama halls and fossil halls as well as the Rose Center for Earth and Space and the Hayden Planetarium. The Museum's scientific collections, only a tiny fraction of which are on view, contain more than 33 million specimens and artifacts. These collections are an invaluable resource for the Museum's 200 scientists, for graduate students in the Museum's Richard Gilder Graduate School—the only museum-based PhD-granting program in the Western Hemisphere—and for researchers around the world.

Visit amnh.org

Drawing of the Museum, 1926, by John Russell Pope, from a hand-colored lantern slide.

CONTENTS

MYTHIC UNICORN
The *Mythic Creatures*
exhibition at the
American Museum of
Natural History featured
a "life-size" model of
a fantastical unicorn,
flooded with pink light.

MYTHIC CREATURES

What was a scientific institution like the American Museum of Natural History up to when it mounted an exhibition called *Mythic Creatures: Dragons, Unicorns, and Mermaids*? *Mythic Creatures* is, first and foremost, a celebration of our capacity as *Homo sapiens sapiens* to imagine the unseen, to make epic tales and fashion homespun folklore, to construct from travelers' tales—and initially inexplicable zoological fragments—things that are fantastic, scary, and sometimes very funny. The final wall of our Anne and Bernard Spitzer Hall of Human Origins includes a celebration of human creativity captured on film: from rituals to tap dance, from students in a classroom to opera. For the duration of the *Mythic Creatures* run at the American Museum of Natural History, it was possible to imagine an invisible thread connecting this montage of human brain and body work to the dragons, unicorns, mermaids, and other mythic creatures realized in story, theater, art, and craft on exhibit in the fourth-floor gallery. The frame of the exhibit was very broad, and we drew on collections from many different places, but for me, it was an opportunity to do some dragon hunting in our own storage.

Dragons, of course, were central to traditional Chinese cosmology. Chinese civilization depended on the productivity of farmers who relied on seasonal rain. On the fifth day of the fifth lunar month, the dragon king would rise up to heaven from his watery palace and release the timely rain. We could show the dragon king and the sea creatures that populated his watery court. These came to us

FISH SHADOW PUPPET
One of the shadow puppets collected for the American Museum of Natural History by Berthold Laufer (see also pages 61, 109, 115, and 150). These nineteenth-century puppets are made of donkey hide, iron, cotton, dye, and tung oil. Shadow puppet shows were once performed on the streets of Beijing.

COLUMBUS An engraving from 1554 titled *Columbus, Discoverer of the West Indies*, by renowned Belgian printmaker Theodor de Bry, depicts Italian explorer Christopher Columbus encountering an ocean full of merpeople and sea monsters upon his arrival in the New World.

in a set of shadow puppets collected in Beijing in 1901 for the Museum by the sinologist Berthold Laufer.

The shadow is an appropriate metaphor for some of the mythic creatures we present, creatures whose shapes in tales and graphic illustrations were the distorted shadows of other things that were really there. The kraken, a sea monster capable of crushing a sailing ship, was imagined from the tentacles of an almost-as-fantastic giant squid, rarely glimpsed because these nonaggressive creatures lurk at great depths. In planning the exhibit, some of our work was inspired by classical folklorist Adrienne Mayor, who has suggested that ancient

Greeks imagined the Cyclops from a pachyderm skull, with its tusk slot in a position that suggested a giant eyehole. In the Gobi desert, ancient sightings of horned *Protoceratops* fossils might have provoked tales of winged griffins guarding golden treasure under the sand.

The source of a mythic creature's shadow might be something else entirely, but the imagination seizes a powerful image to fill in the blanks. Medieval Europeans enthusiastically purchased luminous white "unicorn horns" for their fabled medical properties. These were actually the tusks of narwhals, a northern whale hunted by enterprising Danish sailors. Other large sea mammals such as dugongs and manatees, glimpsed at a distance by sailors too long from land, may have given rise to reported sightings of mermaids combing their long and lustrous hair. Mermaids embody the idea of beauty and danger. Perhaps the mermaid took shape in the imaginings of these sailors, adrift in a world of men on the dangerous ocean and fantasizing about the beautiful and possibly dangerous women in foreign ports. In 1493, Christopher Columbus and his crew sailed close enough to a group of manatees for the navigator to report that, counter to expectation, they were very masculine in their appearance. Similarly, in the late thirteenth century, Marco Polo met the unicorn in the form of a

NARWHAL TUSK An early drawing of a narwhal skull, showing the unusual and unique modified tooth that was often looked at as physical proof of the unicorn's existence. From *Museum Wormianum* (1655), a book by Danish physician Ole Worm on his natural history collection.

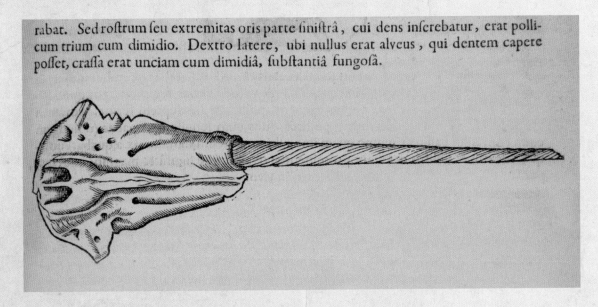

rabat. Sed roſtrum ſeu extremitas oris parte ſiniſtrâ, cui dens inſerebatur, erat polli-
cum trium cum dimidio. Dextro latere, ubi nullus erat alveus, qui dentem capere
poſſet, craſſa erat unciam cum dimidiâ, ſubſtantiâ fungoſâ.

BARONG KET MASK
(Above) Detail of a
Barong Ket mask from a
costume commissioned
by the American
Museum of Natural
History and made by the
male members of Ubud
village in Bali in 2011
(see full costume
on page 60).

Sumatran rhino and reported—with disappointment verging on disgust—that they were ugly, dark, and filthy with mud.

Some sailors saw the mermaid as a lucky talisman and made her a popular form for the figureheads of sailing ships. In this way, long-haired mermaids traveled to new ports and gave a fresh form to local water spirits. In West and Central Africa, the beautiful and dangerous Mami Wata was originally identified with snakes. Snakes remain part of her image, but her body is now that of a mermaid, as West Africans might once have encountered her on the prows of Western ships. In this form, Mami is a foreign beauty, sometimes resembling a Western pinup girl or with an Indian bindi on her forehead, and usually wearing a wristwatch. The water goddess traveled to the New World on slave ships and appears today in mermaid form as Lasirèn in voodoo rituals in Haiti and New York City.

Other times we make our mythic creatures from fragments of other things. No one in Bali has ever encountered the lionlike protective spirit Barong Ket in the deep forest where he is said to reside, and yet every Balinese and most Bali tourists have encountered Barong Ket when he makes a presence in ritual theater. Through the work of culture, a Barong mask is carved in the style of Hindu sculptures and its body costume is inspired by the dancing lions and unicorns used in Chinese celebrations all over Southeast Asia. A priest consecrates the mask and Barong is danced into a village ritual, inhabiting the mask and inspiring the dancers so that when the witch Rangda throws the world into chaos and danger, Barong restores order.

Mythic creatures not only have great staying power, they also morph into available new forms in evolving cultures and inhabit new domains of possible

interaction with us, sometimes in the form of festival masks or as creatures inhabiting video games and Japanese anime. These are domesticated forms of mythic creatures, more playful than likely to provoke fear, but still extremely engaging. While science has unraveled the likely origins of the Cyclops and the griffin, the agile human brain and artful human hand move on to new imaginings.

Laurel Kendall
Curator and Chair of the Division of Anthropology at the
American Museum of Natural History

DANCING LION

A woodblock print
depicting a Japanese lion
dance performance, by
Utamaro, ca. 1789.

Von der Wallschlangen.

Norwegen in stillem Meer/erscheynend Meerschlangē 300. schü
erhaft den schiffleüten/ also daß sy zů zeyten ein menschen auß d
[...]mmend/vnnd das schiff zů grund richtend : erhebend sölche krü
[...]aß auch zů zeyten ein schiff darunder hin faren mag. Sölche ge
[...]aus in seinen Tafeln gesetzt.

INTRODUCTION
MYTHIC CREATURES AT HOME AND IN HISTORY

Before the age of science, myth was how people dealt with the world. If you didn't understand something, you interpreted it with your creative mind—a unique evolutionary development in humans—and probably embellished it quite a bit. You got sick, it was because of a curse hex; saw an animal you didn't know of, it quickly became a fish story; saw molten rock spewing from the earth, an underground fire god was angry.

The focus of the *Mythic Creatures* exhibition that this book is based on is zoology and observation—specifically what the relationship is between our powers of observation and our interpretation of this material.

If we loosely categorize the mythic creature pantheon, there are several commonalities—only rarely do we encounter something really weird, truly unique. Quick examples show that most cultures have myth-based creatures involving giant serpents. Usually these are chimeras of myriad animals patched together to create either something fortunate or something mean and nasty, depending on their cultural context. Giant people, sirens calling men to their deaths, sea serpents, levitating creatures, and water-walking beings also abound around the world. Yet there are very few instances where we can point to detailed physical evidence or real phenomena as the source of these myths. However, I have a couple of favorite examples of real-world phenomena leading to myths, both personal and well known.

One is personal and involves torturing my brother, who is three years younger than me. Already the nascent scientist, I remember a first-grade science experiment about circulation. My teacher showed us that if you put your hands over your ears, you can hear your heart beat in your eardrums. That night in bed, I experienced the same thing when I pressed my ear to my pillow. The light went off, and I immediately put this newfound knowledge to work. I told my brother, Todd, who I shared a room with,

NEW WORLD SEA SERPANTS (Opposite) Detail of a page from a 1575 book by Swiss naturalist Konrad Gesner titled *Fischbuch*. The illustration depicts a giant sea serpent reportedly seen off the coast of Norway and said to be a serpent 120 feet (37 meters) long, large enough to encircle an entire ship and eat sailors whole.

GIANT BIRD OF PERSIA
An illustration of a simurgh—the giant bird of Persian myth that corresponds to the roc—from a seventeenth-century edition of the epic poem *Shahnameh* (Book of Kings). The poem, which is about the history of the Persian empire, was written in the late tenth century by Abu 'l-Qasim Ferdowsi Tusi. Here the simurgh—seen as a wise and benevolent creature—is rescuing an infant who will grow up to be the great Persian warrior king Zāl.

to do the same. He heard something and was scared. I told him that it was a huge army of grotesque beings called the Soup Drummers. The Soup Drummers would come to eat him in his sleep if he slumbered. After a few, actually more than a few, sleepless nights, he told my parents. It didn't scar him into years of therapy, and it is a topic we joke about today. While he thought it was the worst thing that ever happened to him at the time, it is something that he has transmitted to young children in his sphere today—although it doesn't go over as well with parents now as it did in the 1960s! Such is the power of myth, even a spontaneous one, to take an observation that you have no process to explain and interpret in a good (or in this case evil) manner.

Outside of sibling antics, stories of mythic beings and creatures often based on actual—and sometimes extinct—animals abound across the world. One such popular myth is that of the giant bird. The ziz in Jewish culture, the Roc of *The*

Arabian Nights, and the Native American thunderbird immediately come to mind. The Maori have the legendary poukai (see page 105), a large bird that preyed on humans, especially small children. Many large carnivorous birds are illustrated in Maori traditional art, but in 1769, when Captain James Cook became the first European to visit New Zealand (the Dutch explorer Abel Tasman had seen it from his ship in 1642 but could not land), there were no poukai to be seen by Cook's men or later colonists. There was only the oral tradition, some rock art, and a few drawn images. In 1871, archaeologists found the bones of a giant, extinct bird in New Zealand. Some of the subsequent discoveries of "poukai" bones are intermixed with the artifacts of early Maori immigrants.

From these bones, archaeologists have determined that it was a large eagle. Recent DNA analysis has shown that the poukai (now called Haast's Eagle) is closely related to extant regional eagles of Indo-Australia. Estimates of its wingspan are about 30 feet (9 meters) or so, and a maximum weight of around 30 pounds (14 kilograms) is projected. This is very heavy for a flighted animal, and the wingspan is relatively short compared to that of other closely related eagles. This may speak to its hunting style (see page 5).

Before Polynesians made it to New Zealand at the end of the thirteenth century, the entire archipelago was devoid of any mammals except for three species of bats. It did have lots of bird species, and like often occurs on islands without terrestrial mammalian predators, these included several flightless species. The largest land animals in New Zealand pre–human colonization were a flightless group of birds related to ostriches, called moas. The largest adult moa stood near 12 feet (3.6 meters) in height and weighed up to 500 pounds (230 kilograms). Moas were

EXTINCT MOA Illustration of a moa from *Extinct Birds* (1907), by British zoologist Lionel Walter Rothschild, 2nd Baron Rothschild.

月耕隨筆

龍昇天

FUJI DRAGON A colored print titled *Dragon Rising to the Heavens*, 1897, part of a series of prints depicting Mount Fuji by Japanese woodblock artist Ogata Gekkō.

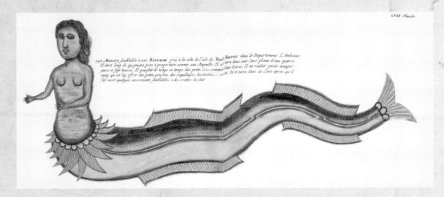

SIREN CALLING

An illustration of a siren from a book printed in Amsterdam by Huguenot publisher Louis Renard, titled *Poissons, écrevisses et crabes de diverses couleurs et figures extraordinaires . . .* , ca. 1678. It shows a "monster resembling a Siren" caught near an island in the Moluccas, an archipelago in Indonesia. The text describes the creature as "59 pouces [inches] (150 cm) long, and in proportion as an eel."

thought to be primary prey for Haast's Eagles. Yet because moas were so big, they weren't carried away by the eagles the way the poukai were said to kidnap young children. Rather, the eagles used their beaks and claws, combined with their weight and velocity, to deliver tremendous blows while diving on unsuspecting moas. Sadly both the Haast's Eagle and the moa became extinct around 1400—about one hundred years after the Maori colonized Polynesia—due to habitat destruction and, in the case of the Haast's Eagle, the elimination of the moa, which was its major food source. The legend of the poukai still exists within the contemporary mythology of the Maori people, and it is a textbook example of how physical sightings and real experience can be incorporated into mythic material that, without the fossil evidence, most non-Maoris would consider pure fantasy.

No matter how we define our ethnicity or culture, mythic creatures dwell somewhere within our psyches. Dragons, almas, jinn, sea serpents of all kinds, enticing maidens, chimeras, and more are still present and real in cultures around the world. Some of these, as is the case of the poukai, actually lived—while the Soup Drummers only exist as an explanation for an unknown phenomenon. But most mythic creatures are just that: myths concocted by a host of experiences and observations expressed through syncretic images and stories. Thousands of these continue to flourish in traditions everywhere.

Mark A. Norell

Macaulay Curator and Chair of the Division of Paleontology at the
American Museum of Natural History

ISLANDIA.

Priuilegio Imp. et Belgico decennali A.º Orteli. excud. 1585

Septemtrio.

Occidens

Moridies.

Scala milliarium Islandicorum.

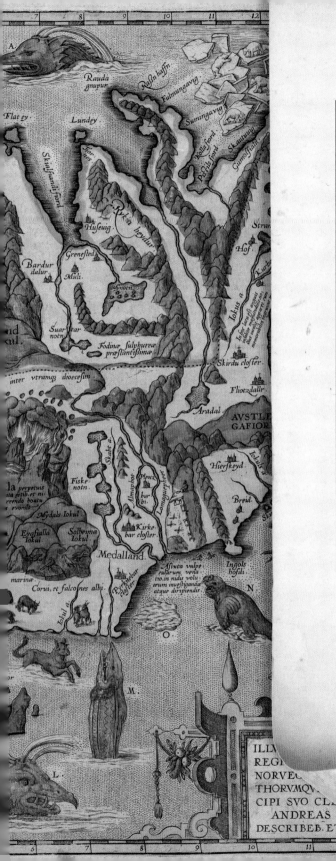

PART 1

WATER

Creatures of the Deep

Water beckons us. It is soothing and seductive, but it's also capable of unleashing deadly force. The mythic creatures that inhabit the depths give form to water's essential mysteries. They arouse feelings of curiosity, hope . . . and bottomless fear. Like water itself, these creatures can be beautiful and enticing. But will they share their life-giving bounty? Or lure us to destruction?

MAP OF ICELAND Several sea monsters cavort in the waters off Iceland in this 1585 map titled *Islandia*, drawn by noted sixteenth-century Flemish cartographer Abraham Ortelius after a map given to him by a Danish historian, Andreas Velleius (Vedel). Shown in the lower left are *vaccae marinae*, the Latin name for "sea cows," and an animal with a horse's head and a fish's tail known as a *hippocampus*.

Chapter 1
SEA MONSTERS

Below the thunders of the upper deep
Far, far beneath in the abysmal sea
His ancient, dreamless, uninvaded sleep
The Kraken sleepeth . . .
There hath he lain for ages and will lie . . .
Until the latter fire shall heat the deep;
Then once by man and angels to be seen,
In roaring he shall rise and on the surface die.

—Alfred, Lord Tennyson,
"The Kraken," 1830

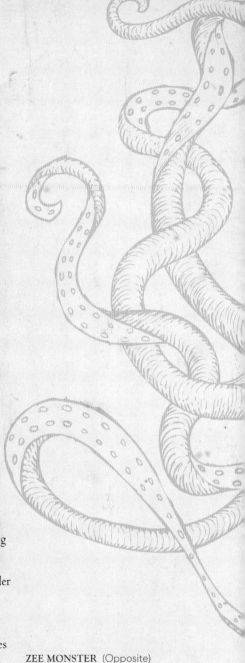

WHY DO PEOPLE SEE SEA MONSTERS? The open ocean can be a terrifying place. Miles from shore on storm-tossed seas, with nothing but water in all directions—including straight down—a sailor or fisherman cannot help but wonder what lurks in the depths. When the oceans were still unexplored, these fears often took the form of imaginary monsters.

Many sea monsters include features of living animals. A large tentacle becomes part of a monstrous sea serpent or a many-armed kraken—the eye sees a fragment, the mind fills in the rest. A blend of tall tales, mistaken identity, and resonant cultural symbols, stories of sea monsters often reveal more about the minds of the imaginers than they do about the natural world.

ZEE MONSTER (Opposite) Sea monsters attack a ship in this engraving by Dutch printmaker Adriaen Collaert, ca. 1594–98.

Many-Armed Monster

Kraken

The mythical kraken may be the largest sea monster ever imagined. Some stories describe it as more than 1.5 miles (2.5 kilometers) around with arms as thick and long as ship masts. Perhaps based on sightings of giant squid tentacles, this multi-armed monster rarely attacked humans, preferring to stay in deep water where it feasted on fish. The chief dangers came from being too close when it surfaced—or too close when it sank, as a boat could be sucked down in the whirlpool created when it submerged.

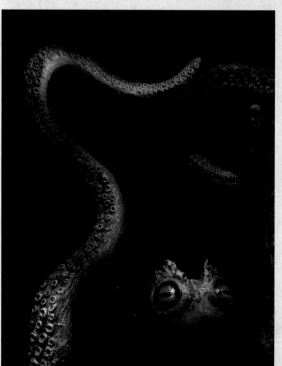

A MODEL OF THE MYTHIC KRAKEN (Left) Hundreds of years ago, European sailors told of a sea monster called the kraken that could toss ships into the air with its many long arms. Today, we know "sea monsters" aren't real—but a living sea animal, the giant squid, has ten arms and can grow longer than a school bus.

LE POULE COLOSSAL (Opposite) A drawing by French naturalist Pierre Dénys de Montfort, 1801, of a giant octopus-like creature attacking a ship off the coast of Angola.

Giant Squid

Five hundred years ago, sailors in northern Europe told of an amazing creature: a monster bigger than a man with numerous long, snakelike arms covered in suckers for grabbing prey. Evidence for this so-called devilfish included bits of giant tentacles found in whale stomachs and vicious battle scars left on the skin of whales by its suckers and claws. Eventually, in the 1850s, scientists recognized the devilfish as an authentic animal—the giant squid.

In 1873, fishermen presented a squid arm—supposedly hacked off the animal when it attacked the men's boat—to the Reverend Moses Harvey, a prominent Canadian naturalist. Harvey wrote about the 19-foot (5.8-meter) long arm:

> I was now the possessor of one of the rarest curiosities in the whole animal kingdom—the veritable tentacle of the hitherto mythical devilfish, about whose existence naturalists had been disputing for centuries. I knew that I held in my hand the key of a great mystery, and that a new chapter would now be added to Natural History.

GIANT SQUID TENTACLE This jar contains a 6-foot (2-meter) section of a tentacle from a giant squid (*Architeuthis kirkii*). The complete specimen was caught by fishermen near New Zealand in 1997 and shipped frozen in ice to the American Museum of Natural History in New York. The entire animal measured 25 feet (7.5 meters), which is not even big by giant squid standards: some can grow to about 70 feet (20 meters).

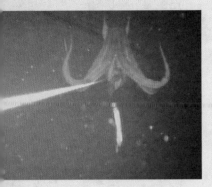

FIRST PHOTO (Above)
Until recently, no giant squid had ever been photographed alive in the depths. But in September 2005, deep in the Pacific Ocean off the coast of Japan, a 25-foot (8-meter) giant squid seized a baited line, triggering an automatic camera that snapped more than five hundred pictures. When the squid finally wrestled free, it left behind a torn-off tentacle. The 18-foot (5.5-meter) long severed limb was still moving when it was hauled on board.

CAPTURED? (Right)
This nineteenth-century engraving shows a giant squid that was said to have been caught by the crew of the French steamer *Alecton* in November 1861.

WHAT'S BIGGER THAN A GIANT SQUID?

THE GIANT SQUID IS not the biggest squid. Scientists have known of an even larger species since at least 1925, but no adult specimen had been found in one piece until 2007, when fishermen hauled one up near New Zealand. Dubbed the "colossal squid," it is thought to be the largest living creature without a backbone. Classified in its own genus, *Mesonychoteuthis hamiltoni* outweighs all of the eight giant squid species in the genus *Architeuthis*.

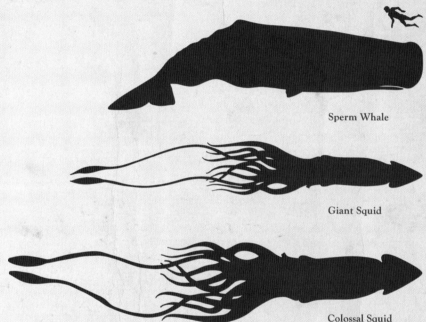

Sperm Whale

Giant Squid

Colossal Squid

"It was a giant squid 25 feet long. It was heading toward the Nautilus, swimming backward very fast. . . . We could clearly make out the 250 suckers lining the inside of its tentacles, some of which fastened onto the glass panel of the lounge. The monster's mouth—a horny beak like that of a parakeet—opened and closed vertically. . . . What a whim of nature! A bird's beak in a mollusk!"

—Jules Verne, *Twenty Thousand Leagues Under the Sea*, 1870

Discovering Monsters

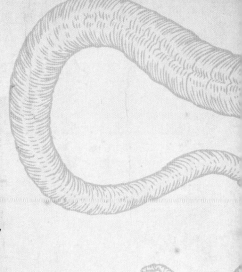

The period from the 1400s to the 1600s in Europe is sometimes called the Age of Exploration. Adventurers set sail from Western Europe seeking wealth, power—and knowledge. When explorers like Christopher Columbus set out on their voyages of discovery, they were literally sailing into uncharted waters. Sea monsters were a concern for them, and frightening rumors ran rampant. Sailors' tales were sometimes the only firsthand information available about ocean animals. These stories ranged from accurate observations to honest mistakes to outright tall tales, with no way for even the most objective naturalist to separate fact from fiction. The meticulous drawings of sea monsters in European natural history books from the 1500s and 1600s reveal the overlap between science and legend at that time.

SEA SERPENTS UNMASKED? Several pictures of sea serpents on old maps appear to be based on sightings of the oarfish, or ribbonfish (*Regalecus glesne*, seen at left). A long, eel-shaped fish that grows to 36 feet (11 meters), the oarfish has a crest of bright red spines on its head and a spiny dorsal fin running down its entire back. Below, an engraving by W. D. Munro from 1860, titled "The Great Serpent, found in Hungry Bay, Bermuda, on January 22, 1860."

Le monstre marin ayant façon d'un moyne.

Before then, Europeans who wrote and illustrated natural history books based them mostly on older books, often deferring to Greek masters such as Aristotle. But as a new view of knowledge arose in Europe emphasizing firsthand observation, information from traveling naturalists became increasingly important. In this transitional era, an author might present a newly discovered animal on the same page as a mythical creature.

Many sincere sea serpent sightings were later debunked as cases of mistaken identity. For instance, several "sea monster" carcasses turned out to be partially decayed basking sharks, an immense fish that grows to 30 feet (9 meters). Other examples of mistaken identity include a "baby sea serpent" that proved to be a deformed blacksnake, and enormous serpents that turned out to be masses of floating seaweed.

FISH BOOK (Above) Among the most startling depictions of sea creatures from books of the 1500s are the "sea monk" and "sea bishop." The former is illustrated here in *La nature & diversité des poissons . . .* (*The Nature and Diversity of Fishes*), 1555, by Pierre Belon. Supposedly captured in Denmark and Germany, these mysterious sea creatures have body parts that mimic the characteristic robes and bishop's hats of Catholic clergymen.

PARALLEL UNIVERSE (Right) This picture from Belon's 1555 book shows a hippocampus, a sea creature with a horse's head and a fish's body. According to a theory popular at that time, every animal found on land had its counterpart in the ocean.

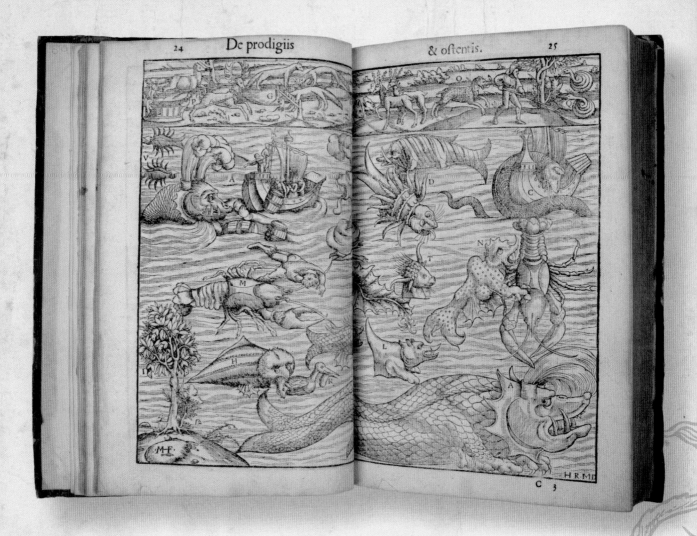

BOOK OF SEA LIFE (Above) Konrad Lykosthenes, a German encyclopedia writer, published this book in Basel, Switzerland, in 1557, titled *Prodigiorum ac Ostentorum Chronicon*. The illustration on the open pages here show the variety of dangerous monsters awaiting sailors on the open seas, including an oversized lobster shown spearing a man with its antenna (labeled *M*). Although these monsters are fanciful, many include elements of real animals.

JONAH AND THE SEA MONSTER? (Following pages) This print by Antonie Wierix, ca. 1585, depicts a scene from the biblical story of Jonah and the whale. The book of Jonah from the Old Testament describes the tribulations of the prophet Jonah, who disobeyed God and sacrificed himself by throwing himself overboard a ship into the sea. Jonah was saved when swallowed by an enormous whale or fish and, after three days of prayer, was spit out onto dry land. In many early images, such as this print, and especially in medieval iconography, the biblical whale is typically depicted as a sea monster or serpent.

NESSIE Stories that appeal to the imagination are hard to dispel—especially when there is no way to disprove them. Take the Loch Ness monster—seen here in a contemporary photomontage—which is said to inhabit a lake in northern Scotland. Though investigators have searched for the monster with underwater cameras and sonar for decades—and some alleged evidence was exposed as a fraud—people still flock to the site, hoping for a glimpse of "Nessie."

"On the 6th of July 1734, when off the south coast of Greenland, a sea-monster appeared to us, whose head, when raised, was on level with our main-top. Its snout was long and sharp, and it blew water almost like a whale; it had large broad paws; its body was covered with scales; its skin was rough and uneven; in other respects it was as a serpent; and when it dived, its tail, which was raised in the air, appeared to be a whole ship's length from its body."

—Hans Egede, Norwegian missionary,
later bishop of Greenland

SERPENT OR DOLPHIN?

COULD ROWS OF LEAPING whales, seals, or dolphins (like the picture shown at bottom) have inspired tales of sea serpents? In 1872, Captain A. Hassel reported seeing an "immense serpent" with "four fins on its back" about 200 feet (61 meters) from his ship near Galveston, Texas. A member of his crew drew the illustration on the top. It is easy to see how a line of dolphins (*Delphinus delphis*) might be mistaken for a single giant serpent.

REGIO
DE
BRASIL

Oegliano
Rio de Maraf mor

La Trinital

A. Scenson

Islas de Martin vaes

Isolas di S. Maria lagosto

Punta segura
Rio de m george
S. Toma
S. Salvador
Baxos de vargas
Cabo de los baxos
Golfo de los reys

Cabo S. Agostin
Rio s. Francesco
Rio Real
Rio de todos Santos
Rio de S. Agostin
Acenson
Rio de la urgines
La Trinidad

Rio de brasil
Rio de Cosmos

R. deuhay
Playa llana
Rio sulfonae
R. S. Frackesco
R. datteon
Po de Don
rodrigo
R. poplado
Rio igual

La cananea
S. Catalna

del riparo

de S. Maria
Rio de la plata
Islas de Ko Aluares
Ysla di Xpoual iggues

de Saison

OCEANVS
AVSTRALIS

Crispisiolo
Y. de Cersealna

Golfo de S Bassano

Mutating Myths

When European settlers came to Australia and the Americas, they brought stories—and learned new ones from the people already there. Some of these stories were about frightening monsters and powerful spirits. While some scoffed at these tales, others told and retold the stories themselves.

People's beliefs are often changed by contact with other cultures. Missionaries, for instance, work to convince others to give up their previous beliefs. But old stories don't just disappear. More often, they survive and blend with new ideas—and sometimes it is the newcomers who adopt local beliefs.

One interesting question to consider in regard to these myths is this: can mythic creatures become extinct? All mythic creatures are mysterious. We often do not know exactly where their stories came from, what they mean, or why they appeal to us so much. The best way to get answers about myths and other stories is to ask the people who tell them. But what if all those people are gone, their songs and stories silent forever? And what if there is no written record of the culture that produced a mythic creature? Anthropologists, archaeologists, and psychologists can offer powerful theories and profound insights by studying artifacts. But in many cases, the ultimate answer for questions about myths is: we will never know for certain.

MAP (Opposite) A detail from a 1562 map titled *Americae Sive Qvartae Orbis Partis Nova et Exactissima Descriptio* (*A New and Most Exact Description of America or the Fourth Part of the World*), by Hieronymus Cock of Antwerp (ca. 1510–70). On the bottom left, off the coast of South America, a merman atop a large sea monster holds the royal coat of arms of Spain, surrounded by other sea monsters, fish, ships, and another merman.

KILLER WHALE TRUMPET (Right) The picture on this ceramic trumpet from Peru (300 BCE to 800 CE) shows the Nazca mythic killer whale (see page 26). It differs from an ordinary whale in that it has arms and multiple dorsal fins. It is shown here holding a human head.

• Australian Aborigines
once told of bunyips
with sharp tusks that ate
people. But as fear of
bunyips lessened, they
were often described as
grazing animals.

• Bunyips are mostly
said to have shaggy
fur—but some are
described with scales or
feathers.

• They are supposedly
the size of a small cow.

• They may have flippers
for swimming, which
change to legs to walk
on land at night.

BUNYIP

According to legend, a man-eating monster called the bunyip once lived in the rivers, lakes, and swamps of Australia. Its howl carried through the night air, making people afraid to enter the water. At night, the bunyip prowled the land, hunting for women and children to eat.

Over time, as European settlers retold this Aboriginal story, it became less frightening and its meaning changed; in the 1800s people used the word as an insult meaning "imposter." The bunyip became a plant-eater, not a man-eater, and it now often appears as a friendly creature in children's books.

BUNYIP OR NOT? (Above) Fascinated by Australian stories of the bunyip, some colonists mistook large, unfamiliar skulls for bunyip skulls. In 1846, the Australian Museum in Sydney exhibited a "bunyip" skull found at the Murrumbidgee River. The discovery so stirred the popular imagination that, according to the *Sydney Morning Herald*, "almost everyone became immediately aware that he had heard 'strange sounds' from the lagoons at night, or had seen 'something black' in the water." The skull shown above, in a drawing reproduced in the *Tasmanian Journal of Natural Science*, ca. 1846, was later determined to have come from a deformed horse.

MAN-EATER (Left) An illustration of a bunyip from a story in Andrew Lang's *The Brown Fairy Book*, 1910.

"In 1847, the Sydney Morning Herald reported an eyewitness encounter between a herdsman and a bunyip. The man said it was as big as a calf, with 'large ears which it pricked up when it perceived him; had a thick mane of hair from the head down the neck, and two large tusks. He turned to run away, and this creature equally alarmed ran off too {with} an awkward shambling gallop.'"

FOSSIL RECORD Fossils of *Diprotodon*, a grazing marsupial that lived in Australia until about 10,000 years ago (shown below in a modern illustration), were sometimes interpreted as the remains of bunyips.

- The killer whale is just one of many mythic creatures depicted on Nazca pottery; others look like birds, monkeys, serpents, and people.

- The mythical killer whale has more fins on its back than an actual whale.

- Often shown with hands instead of fins.

- Carries a human head, but is not necessarily evil; the Nazca people of Peru themselves collected human skulls. Were they headhunters? Were they tending their own ancestors?

NAZCA KILLER WHALE

A killer whale . . . clutching a human head? The ancient people known today as the Nazca painted this startling creature on their pottery (see page 23) and carved enormous outlines of it into the ground. Who is this beast? What does it do with the human heads it carries? No one knows.

The Nazca people lived along the west coast of South America in what is now Peru from around 1 CE until about 700 CE. Then they disappeared. Their colorful ceramics are covered with puzzling images such as the mythical killer whale—but there is no one left to explain what these images mean.

DOUBLE-SPOUTED BOTTLE (Below left) This ceramic vessel from Peru, 300 BCE to 800 CE, is shaped like the Nazca mythic killer whale. During the seven centuries from 1 to 700 CE, Nazca ceramics passed through eight different styles. Since the imagery the Nazca used changed over time, whatever symbolic meanings might apply to a mythic killer whale likely changed over time as well.

THE NAZCA LINES The most famous Nazca creations are immense patterns of lines carved into the ground; they are still visible today. The lines form mysterious patterns and pictures so large that they cannot be seen from the ground—and so were most likely never seen in full by the Nazca people themselves. Many of these giant pictures depict the same creatures shown on Nazca pottery, including the mythical killer whale shown here. At various times these lines were thought to be roads, a giant calendar, and even landing sites for spaceships—theories that have all been largely discarded.

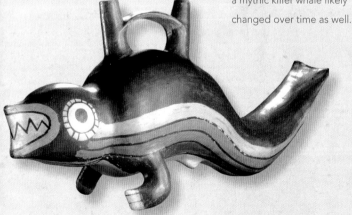

"In 1529, the Spanish monk Fra Bernardino da Sahagún went to Mexico to convert the Aztecs to Christianity. He kept detailed records of Aztec stories, including a long description of Ahuizotl. His goal was not to preserve these stories, but to stamp out the beliefs associated with them: 'For how are we priests to preach against idolatrous practices, superstitious observances, abuses, and omens, if we are not acquainted with these?'"

AHUIZOTL

Crying at night like a baby, the doglike creature called Ahuizotl (ah-wee-ZO-tul) was said to lure people to their deaths. The Aztecs of Mexico told of how Ahuizotl lived at the bottom of deep pools of water. It had hands and feet like a monkey and a long, coiled tail with a hand on the end. When people responded to the cries of the weeping child, Ahuizotl grabbed them with the hand on its tail and pulled them down into the water. A few days later, the victim's body would float to the surface, missing only the eyes, teeth, and nails.

Ahuizotl Facts

• Aztec stories of Ahuizotl describe the creature as the size of a dog and having pointed ears.

• Hands and feet like a monkey or raccoon and a long, flexible tail with a hand on the end.

• Ahuizotl would cry like a baby to lure people near the water where it lived, and then pull them under.

AHUIZOTL CARVING In 1502, this stone carving of Ahuizotl was set into a wall of an Aztec temple near Tepoztlán, Mexico. This picture of the legendary creature is actually a pictographic symbol. It represents the Aztec ruler Ahuitzotl, an ambitious military leader who seized vast new lands for his empire between 1486 and 1502.

TAMING MONSTERS

HOW DO MYTHIC CREATURES FARE IN THE MODERN WORLD?

When old stories enter the modern world, many once-frightening legends are softened, reflecting the modern desire to preserve childhood innocence. Mythic animals that once were scary may become cute and cuddly. In Japan, for instance, a creature called the *kappa* was long known for pulling children underwater and drowning them. Today, Japanese children are more familiar with a cute, friendly kappa that appears in consumer products such as toys, movies, and children's books.

Traditionally, the kappa was said to be the size of a child but stronger than a man. It had a face like a monkey but with a beak; green, scaly skin and a shell like a turtle; webbed hands and feet; and smelled like fish.

Children in Japan were once taught to be careful when swimming in rivers and ponds, lest a kappa drag them underwater. Because kappas love to eat cucumbers, parents used to write their children's names on cucumbers and throw them into the water as gifts, so the kappa would not drown their children when they went swimming.

TRADITIONAL KAPPA A Japanese painting of a kappa from the *Kaikidan Ekotoba* monster scroll, mid-nineteenth century.

Water carried in a bowl-shaped dent in its head is its source of power. When a kappa leaves the water, its strength depends on this water it carries on its head. When bothered by a kappa, a person should bow to it. Forced by politeness to bow back, the kappa will spill the water on its head and lose its power, forcing it to run back to its river or pond.

KAPPA MASK Kappa masks are sometimes worn in festivals or used as decoration. This papier-mâché and fiber mask was sold in a modern temple market in Tokyo, Japan. The face suggests a friendly, childlike kappa.

KAPPA NETSUKE Tiny wood and ivory sculptures, called *netsuke*, were originally used as toggles to secure small containers or pouches to clothing, often a kimono. Made since the 1600s, netsuke are now prized by collectors. The one shown here has hitched a ride on the back of a clam.

MODERN KAPPA

The kappa is still very much a part of life in modern Japan. Many common phrases refer to kappas:

- *Kappa maki*: cucumber sushi rolls (because kappas love cucumbers)

- *Okappa*: bobbed hairstyle

- *Kappa*: straw raincoat, which somewhat resembles a kappa shell

- *Kappa no Kawa Nagare*: "even a kappa can drown," indicating that even an expert can make mistakes

- *Kappa no He*: much ado about nothing ("just a kappa fart")

- *Kappa Mikey*: TV cartoon in United States and Japan (name probably comes from kappa maki—see above)

- Kappa Bridge in Tokyo

Chapter 2

BECOMING MERMAIDS

The waters rush'd, the waters rose,
A fisherman sat by,

And, lo! a dripping mermaid fair
Sprang from the troubled main.

She sang to him, to him spake she,
His doom was fix'd, I ween;
Half drew she him, and half sank he,
And ne'er again was seen.

--Johann Wolfgang von Goethe,
"The Fisherman," 1808

WHY DO SO MANY WATER SPIRITS LOOK LIKE MERMAIDS? Many people around the world tell of water creatures that are half-fish and half-human. Although these creatures are all different, sometimes they have odd details in common. For example, mermaids in Europe, Africa, and the Americas are typically depicted carrying combs and mirrors. This detail was passed from Europe to Africa to the Americas as merchants and slaves spread mermaid stories and art around the world. And in many cases, water spirits that weren't originally mermaids took on that form only after images of mermaids were introduced by outsiders.

MERMAID ENGRAVING
(Opposite) An illustration by Dutch engraver Egidius Sadeler called *Fable of the Mermaid*, 1608.

European Mermaids

In European stories, mermaids were thought to be beautiful, seductive, and dangerous—like the sea itself. They could bring good luck or bad. Ship figureheads were sometimes carved in the shape of mermaids. Some sailors also carved mermaids from walrus ivory and whale teeth, but many avoided carving mermaids, fearing that would bring bad luck. Throughout history, many Europeans have testified to the existence of mermaids, and some have even claimed to have seen them personally. Some of these sightings are noted on the map (see pages 34–35).

MIRROR, MIRROR (Left) Two mermaids hold mirrors in this detail from Hieronymus Cock's 1562 map *Americae Sive Qvartae Orbis Partis . . .* (*America or the Fourth Part of the World*).

SURVIVING THE FLOOD (Opposite) This picture from the Nuremberg Bible of 1483 shows a mermaid swimming near Noah's ark. According to this illustration of the biblical story of the Flood, when land animals were rescued in the ark, the merfolk stayed nearby to weather the storm.

MERMAID SIGHTINGS MAP

20TH-CENTURY SIGHTINGS Mermaid sightings were reported in Ireland as recently as 1910, when one was seen in County Clare. One local said that mermaids were a bad omen, because the last sighting in 1849 was followed by the Great Famine.

AMERICAN MERMAIDS English explorer Captain John Smith, famous for his legendary encounter with his Powhatan rescuer, Pocahontas, claimed in 1614 that he saw a fish-tailed mermaid with round eyes, a finely shaped nose, well-formed ears, and long green hair. The creature, he said, was "by no means unattractive."

MERMAID OR MANATEE? In the ocean near Haiti in 1493, Christopher Columbus—probably glimpsing a manatee—reported seeing three mermaids but said they were "not as pretty as they are depicted, for somehow in the face they look like men."

ACCORDING TO EXPERTS The Roman writer Pliny the Elder was a scientific authority whose thirty-seven-volume *Natural History*, completed in 77 CE, was consulted for over a thousand years. Yet Pliny wrote that mermaids were "no fabulous tale . . . look how painters draw them, so they are indeed."

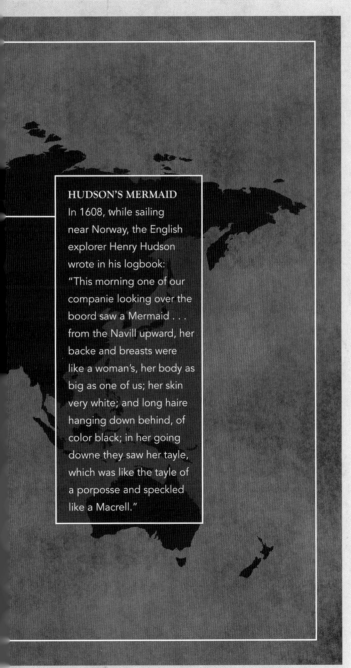

HUDSON'S MERMAID

In 1608, while sailing near Norway, the English explorer Henry Hudson wrote in his logbook: "This morning one of our companie looking over the boord saw a Mermaid . . . from the Navill upward, her backe and breasts were like a woman's, her body as big as one of us; her skin very white; and long haire hanging down behind, of color black; in her going downe they saw her tayle, which was like the tayle of a porposse and speckled like a Macrell."

THE LITTLE MERMAID (Above) In 1836, the Danish author Hans Christian Andersen adapted the mermaid story into one of its most memorable forms, *The Little Mermaid*, a tragic tale of a young mermaid who gives up her voice to walk on land. This illustration is from an 1899 book of Hans Christian Andersen's fairy tales, illustrated by Helen Stratton.

MERMAID FIGUREHEAD (Above opposite) A wooden mermaid from the prow of an early 1900s American ship.

MERMAID WITH SNAKE (Above) Detail of *The Water*,
by Dutch engraver Philip Galle, after Marcus Gheeraerts,
ca. 1547; the mermaid is shown holding a snake, as does
the African mermaid Mami Wata (see next page).

CITY SYMBOL (Left) The Mermaid, or Syrenka, of Warsaw
has been the symbol of Poland's capital city since the
Middle Ages. This statue (a cast of the original) stands in
the Old Town Square in Warsaw; the original was sculpted
in bronze by Konstanty Hegel in 1855.

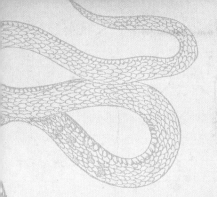

African and Caribbean Mermaids

Mami Wata
Facts

• Mami Wata has
followers in over twenty
countries in West,
Central, and Southern
Africa.

• Long, straight hair.

• Often shown with
a mirror and comb,
symbols for beauty
and vanity.

• Sometimes depicted
in modern, foreign
clothes, and often
wearing a watch.

• Holds a snake (before
the mermaid image
became popular, many
African water spirits
were depicted as snakes).

• Mami Wata sometimes
lures people underwater
to their deaths—
although some come
back as her mediums
with special powers.

• People often paint
pictures of Mami Wata
on lottery parlor walls
for luck.

Mami Wata

Mami Wata is one of the most popular—and powerful—African water spirits. She is most often portrayed as a mermaid, although she has other forms. Mami Wata heals the sick and brings good luck to her followers. But she also has a temper and will drown people who don't obey her. She will cause confusion, sickness, and visions in those she calls to serve her as mediums. Many followers seek her help by dancing until they enter a trance. Her name comes from the English words "mammy water," and it is fitting that she has a foreign name, since followers believe she comes from another world, the world of the sea.

Hundreds of years ago, numerous water spirits were said to live in West Africa. In stories told by the Igbo people and others, some water spirits were half fish, half human, but many looked like snakes or crocodiles. In the 1500s, ships with statues of mermaids on their prows began arriving from Europe. These strangers came from the sea, like the Africans' water spirits. Could the mermaids on these ships be carvings of water spirits?

Over time, the European mermaid legend blended with local stories, and more and more Africans came to portray their water spirits as half woman, half fish. Many of these stories merged into one, so the most powerful water spirit in many African countries is now known as Mami Wata.

WATER SPIRIT (Opposite)
Punch-decorated brass tray
with a Mami Wata image,
from the Efik peoples of
southeast Nigeria, mid-to-
late nineteenth century.

MAMI WATA (Right)
A wall painting of Mami
Wata in the Volta region
of Ghana.

LASIRÈN

The mermaid Lasirèn is a powerful water spirit popular in the Caribbean islands and parts of the Americas. Like European mermaids and the African mermaid water spirit Mami Wata, Lasirèn holds a mirror to admire herself and a comb for her long, straight hair. Lasirèn's underwater world is known as "the back of the mirror," and her mirror is a symbol of the boundary between the two worlds. Followers of Lasirèn say she takes them below the water to her world, and they return with new powers. Some women become voodoo priestesses this way.

The story of Lasirèn blends African and European mermaid stories with Caribbean culture. When African slaves were brought to the Caribbean, they took their stories with them. In Haiti, Lasirèn is part of the voodoo tradition, and her followers appeal to her for help in ceremonies, where the mermaid's spirit may enter the body of a female follower and bring good luck with work, health, money, and love.

Lasirèn is one of three powerful female water spirits, sometimes considered sisters, who are honored in Haitian shrines. One sister is cool, calm, and seductive. Another is hot, passionate, angry, and strong. Lasirèn's personality is a blend of these opposites. Together, they validate a wide range of temperaments for women.

MODERN LASIRÈN
A mosaic bottle-cap sculpture called *La Siren II* by American artist John T. Unger, made in 2004.

DANGEROUS AND ALLURING

THE NAME LASIRÈN COMES from the French word *sirène*, meaning "mermaid." In Greek myths, the sirens were bird-women who called out to sailors, luring them to smash their ships on the rocks. In Homer's *Odyssey*, a Greek epic dating to at least 800 BCE, the hero Ulysses ties himself to the mast of his ship so he can resist the sirens. In the last thousand years, the siren story became mixed with the European mermaid story, and mermaids are now sometimes called sirens.

ODYSSEUS A Roman mosaic of Ulysses and the Sirens from the second century CE.

"*The mermaid, the whale,
My hat falls into the sea.
I caress the mermaid,
My hat falls into the sea.
I lie down with the mermaid,
My hat falls into the sea.*"

—Haitian Voodoo chant sung to Lasirèn

Inuit and Aboriginal Mermaids

Sedna Facts

• Inuit sea goddess, based on an early Inuit story of a vengeful daughter.

• She is honored as the mother of sea mammals and the guardian spirit of the Inuit.

• She is supposedly the size of a small cow.

• Did not assume her mermaid form until Western whalers arrived in the Arctic.

SEDNA

The story of Sedna is one of the most dramatic tales of the Inuit people, who live in the Arctic regions of Alaska, Canada, and Greenland. In a deadly tale of betrayal on the stormy sea, a young woman is tossed overboard by her own father, yet she survives to create the whales, seals, and walruses on which the Inuit depend for food and materials. Today, Sedna is often depicted as a mermaid, but this was not always the case. Before whalers came to the Arctic, most stories said she looked like a human or they didn't describe her appearance at all. Stories of creatures who were half woman, half fish—the mermaid form that could be seen on many of the arriving ships—became associated with Sedna in Inuit art. Many related stories about Inuit sea goddesses are told in different regions, using several names besides Sedna. These stories can be comforting—such as those about the gentle mother sea goddess Taleelajuq—or terrifying, like the story of Sedna (see opposite page).

SEDNA This large Sedna, with her long braids flowing above her head, was carved by Pitseolak Niviaksi in 1991. Notably, Sedna has webbed fingers in this carving. In the traditional telling of the story, Sedna's human fingers were chopped off. Falling into the sea, her fingers became the seals, walruses, and whales.

GIFT FROM THE SEA

THE STORY OF SEDNA is violent and sad—yet it tells of the greatest gifts the Inuit ever received. Like any story told and retold for hundreds of years, there are many versions. The one here is based on a version published in 1885 by Franz Boas, an anthropologist from the American Museum of Natural History. Boas traveled around lower Baffin Island to study the Inuit, who were then called "Eskimos."

THE STORY OF SEDNA

An Inuit man lived alone with his daughter, Sedna, who refused to marry. At last a bird promised her a life of comfort in a land over the sea, and they married. But the bird lied; Sedna's new life was filled with cold and hunger. When her father visited, a year later, she begged him to take her home. So he killed the bird and they set out to sea.

THE WORLD OF THE INUIT The Inuit live in a harsh Arctic environment and depend on animals from the sea for food and materials. These animals are said to have been provided by Sedna.

The bird's friends whipped up a giant storm with their wings. Fearing they would drown, Sedna's father threw her overboard to save himself. Sedna clung to the boat. So her father cut off the tips of her fingers, which became seals. Still Sedna hung on, so her father cut her fingers off at the knuckles. These pieces became walruses. Finally he cut off the stumps of her fingers, which turned into whales, and she sank into the sea.

Amazingly, she did not drown. When the sea calmed, her father let her back into the boat. But Sedna swore revenge, and when home, she made her dogs chew off her father's hands and feet. Her father put a curse on them all, and the earth opened and swallowed them. Since then, they have lived in the underworld. Sedna is now honored as the mother of all the sea mammals and the guardian spirit of the Inuit.

- Yawkyawks live in water holes where the creative force that made the world is still strong; they use this power to bring rain and help people have babies.

- Yawkyawks take many forms besides mermaids; some have parts of crocodiles, swordfish, or snakes.

- If you see strings of seaweed or green algae in the water, it may be a Yawkyawk's hair.

- Australian Aborigines in various regions use different names for the Yawkyawk, including Ngalberddjen, Ngalkunburruyaymi, Djómi, and Jin-gubardabiya.

- Yawkyawks may marry humans, but such marriages can end suddenly when the Yawkyawk decides to return to the water.

Yawkyawk

In Australia, the Aboriginal people speak of ancient spirits that made the land, trees, and animals and that still live in sacred water holes. Some of these spirit beings, called Yawkyawks, look like mermaids: young women with fish tails and long hair resembling strings of seaweed or green algae. Some people say these creatures grow legs at night to walk on land or even fly around in the form of dragonflies. Yawkyawks have the power to give life—just going near a Yawkyawk's water hole can make a woman pregnant. They provide drinking water and rain so plants can grow, but if angry, they may bring storms.

In other countries, water spirits took the form of mermaids only after that story arrived from Europe, but in Australia, the Yawkyawk already resembled a mermaid before Europeans arrived. Sometimes a story or image travels from one country to the next, but other times people just come up with similar stories on their own.

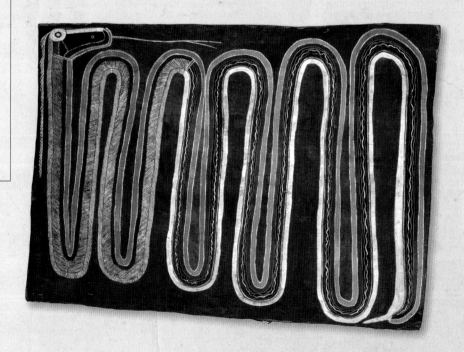

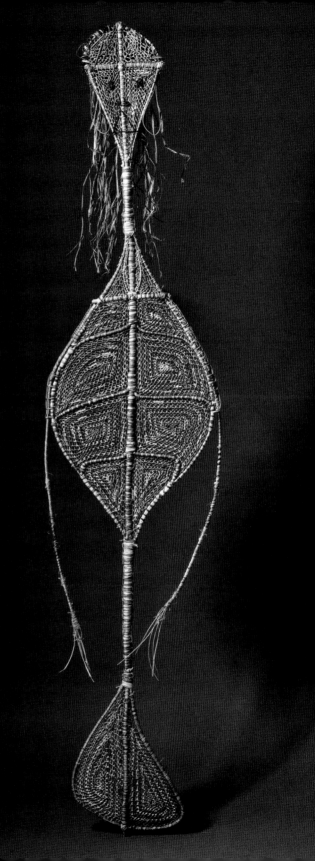

A COMPLICATED RELATIONSHIP

(Opposite) A creator spirit of the Australian Aborigines is a rainbow serpent named Ngalyod, depicted here in a bark painting from the second half of the twentieth century. He is linked to the Yawkyawk spirit, but their relationship varies among different groups of people in different regions. Some say the Yawkyawk is his daughter, some say they are a couple, and some say they are different forms of the same being.

YAWKYAWK SCULPTURE (Right)

Marina Murdilnga (b.1960) made this Yawkyawk in 2005 from fiber, which is not a traditional medium. Her Yawkyawk figure represents female water spirits who live near the artist's home at Maningrida in Australia's Northern Territory.

FEEJEE MERMAID

Want to make a mermaid? Take the head and torso of a monkey and the tail of a fish and sew them together. People have been making these fake mermaids for at least four hundred years. Created first in the East Indies, hundreds were eventually made for sale to British and American sailors. The most spectacular mermaid hoax was pulled off by the famous showman P. T. Barnum. In 1842, Barnum tricked thousands of people in New York City into paying to see a fake mermaid supposedly caught near the Fiji Islands. The name Feejee mermaid is now used for all such manufactured mermaids.

In 1842, New York newspapers announced that a mermaid had been caught near the Fiji Islands in the Pacific. In fact, circus founder P. T. Barnum had rented the fake mermaid from a fellow museum owner in Boston. To attract an audience for the dried, shriveled monstrosity, Barnum gave out ten thousand handbills with pictures of mermaids that looked like beautiful young girls. Horrified visitors instead found that "the Feejee lady is the very incarnation of ugliness," as one newspaper put it.

In 2005, photographs of phony mermaids circulated widely on the Internet. The manufactured mermaids supposedly washed up on a beach in India in the wake of the devastating tsunami that occurred in the Indian Ocean on December 26, 2004.

FIERY END (Above) A nineteenth-century lithograph titled *Burning of Barnum's Museum*, July 13, 1865, after a painting by American artist Christopher P. Cranch. Barnum's American Museum in New York City burned to the ground in 1865, taking with it, among other exhibits, the Feejee mermaid.

ON VIEW (Right) Illustration of woman viewing the "Feejee mermaid" under glass at an exhibit at the former Boston Museum, from an 1856 guide to Boston.

FEEJEE MERMAID (Opposite) The original Feejee mermaid made famous by P. T. Barnum is believed to have been destroyed in a fire—but some people think this one may be it. More than one hundred years old and made of wood, papier-mâché, wool, and fish bones, it was rediscovered in a museum collection in 1973. Some scholars connect it to Barnum but its exact origins are unknown.

PART 2

LAND

Creatures of the Earth

We share the land with countless living animals. Some are familiar; others seem quite bizarre. Creatures from the lands of myth can be both recognizable and strange. Sometimes they appear to have body parts from ordinary animals combined in very unusual ways. Other times they look just like familiar animals—but have extraordinary and magical powers.

ORDINARY AND EXTRAORDINARY In this work by Dutch painter Paulus Potter, titled *Orpheus Charming the Beasts* (1650), a glowing unicorn is one of the beasts falling under the spell of the legendary Greek musician's lyre.

Cum Privilegio

Chapter 3
ANCIENT MONSTERS

A very remarkable history this is
Of one Polyphemus and Captain Ulysses:
The latter a hero accomplished and bold,
The former a knave, and a fright to behold,—
A horrid big giant who lived in a den,
And dined every day on a couple of men
. . . .
He'd only one eye; . . . a terrible one,—
"As large" (Virgil says) "as the disk of the sun!"

—John Godfrey Saxe,
"Polyphemus and Ulysses," ca. 1873

DO MYTHIC CREATURES HAVE BONES? Imagine walking along a bluff
in ancient Greece and finding a leg bone several times the size of your own. What
would you think? What if you saw a massive, humanlike skull with only a single hole
where the eyes should be? Or a skeleton with four legs and a sharp, curved beak?
What sort of creatures could these be?

Today, scientists recognize such bones as the remains of long-extinct
mammoths, dinosaurs, and other animals. But to many ancient Greeks, these
unfamiliar bones were proof of the existence of the giants, cyclopes, and griffins
that were described in the popular stories and travel accounts of the time.

MYTHIC CYCLOPES

(Opposite) Blacksmith
cyclopes work in the forge of
the Greek god Hephaestus,
in this engraving by Cornelis
Cort after Titian, 1572.

Griffins

Griffinlike creatures appear in the stories of many cultures in North Africa, the Middle East, and Europe. But griffins do not always symbolize the same thing in every culture. In some cases, the griffin became a representation of greed. In others, it was considered to be majestic and noble, like an eagle or lion. Dazzling griffin illustrations date back at least as far as 3300 BCE. Griffins were enormously popular in the artwork of many cultures and especially on European coats of arms in the Middle Ages. Today, griffins can be seen in popular children's movies such as the Chronicles of Narnia series, and books such as *Alice's Adventures in Wonderland*.

Griffin Facts

- Griffins are said to live in nests in the mountains.

- Head, torso, and talons of an eagle or sometimes other beaked birds, like peacocks.

- Body of a lion with four legs—sometimes with a serpent's tail.

- Tawny coat of a lion, spotted fur, or colorful feathers.

- Most griffin descriptions include wings, but not all.

GREEK COIN (Above right) This gold coin depicting a griffin is from what is now the Crimea, Ukraine—once a Greek colony. It is dated ca. 370–350 BCE.

GRIFFIN IN NATURE (Right) A griffin surrounded by flora, engraved by David Loggan in 1663 after an image by noted Bohemian etcher Wenceslaus Hollar.

GRIFFIN STATUE

Powerful mythic creatures are often used as logos for schools, companies, and even sports teams. American wood-carver Joe Leonard made this griffin statue in the 1980s, while working on a similar one for a Pennsylvania high school, whose mascot is a griffin.

"Now the place where the griffins live and the gold is found is a grim and terrible desert. Waiting for a moonless night, the treasure-seekers come with shovels and sacks and dig. If they manage to elude the griffins, the men reap a double reward, for they escape with their lives and bring home a cargo of gold— rich profit for the dangers they face."

—Greek author Aelian, ca. 200 CE

ROMAN STATUETTE (Left) Artists in the ancient world often associated griffins with Nemesis, the Greek goddess of retribution. Here, in this glazed faience statuette from Egypt, ca. 150 CE, a griffin is turning the wheel of fortune that Nemesis uses to decide a person's fate.

"GRIFON" OF INDIA (Below) This illustration is from a 1552 edition of *Cosmographia* by German cartographer Sebastian Münster.

BLUE GRIFFIN This hand-colored pen-and-ink drawing of a lynx and a griffin is from the *Northumberland Bestiary*, ca. 1250.

CITY SYMBOL Griffins were prevalent in the mythology and iconography of the ancient Assyrian Empire; here, a Dutch engraving from ca. 1600 by Adriaen Collaert depicts a griffin accompanying Ninus, who in Greek myth was described as the legendary founder of Nineveh, the capital of the empire.

GUARDING GOBI GOLD

More than two thousand years ago, hardy gold miners sought their fortunes in the vast Gobi Desert of central Asia. These miners were Scythians—members of a horse-riding people who controlled much of central Asia and the northern Middle East between about 800 BCE and 200 CE. Relying on travelers' tales, Greek authors reported that in the scorching heat of the Gobi, the miners battled not only the blazing sun but also the mighty griffin—a fierce half-eagle, half-lion hybrid that guarded fantastic treasures of gold.

Millions of years before humans arrived in the Gobi, some parts of the desert were home to strange animals that seemed to combine body parts of eagles and lions. But these animals weren't griffins—they were dinosaurs. Certain areas in the Gobi are littered with dinosaur bones, including those of the four-legged, beaked *Protoceratops*. Ancient gold miners working in the desert may have seen these fossils—and perhaps based their descriptions of griffins on them.

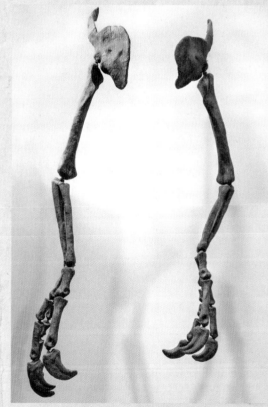

BORROWED BODY PARTS Many different dinosaur fossils found in the Gobi may have contributed to various griffin descriptions. Among these are the enormous claws of *Therizinosaurus* and *Deinocheirus*, which are similar to the griffin claws seen in some depictions.

"We stopped at a low saddle between the hills. Before I could remove the keys from the ignition, Mark sang out excitedly. . . . Several feet away, near the very apex of the saddle, was a stunning skull and partial skeleton of a Proto, a big fellow whose beak and crooked fingers pointed west to our small outcrop, like a griffin pointing the way to a guarded treasure. . . . We continued to pounce on precious specimens with remarkable consistency. . . . Mark would sing out, 'Skull!' and, almost on cue I would find one too. The surface of the gentle slopes and shallow gullies was splattered with white patches [of fossils], as if someone had emptied a paint can in a random fashion over the ground."

—Paleontologist Michael Novacek describing the discovery of *Protoceratops* fossils on an American Museum of Natural History 1993 expedition to the Gobi Desert with fellow paleontologist Mark Norell.

EVIDENCE EVERYWHERE In many parts of the world, dinosaur fossils are incredibly rare and hard to find—but not in certain parts of the Gobi Desert. On an expedition in the Gobi Desert in the 1920s, Roy Chapman Andrews of the American Museum of Natural History found this *Protoceratops* specimen (photograph above) poking out of a hillside. For thousands of years, *Protoceratops* fossils could regularly be seen eroding out of hillsides such as this. In recent years, many have been collected, making them somewhat less common in such landscapes. At right, a specimen from the *Mythic Creatures* exhibition.

BARONG KET

Creatures like the unicorn and griffin sprang from the human imagination to populate myths and legends. Sometimes people can interact with mythic animals when they come to life as part of a play or performance. The hulking, shaggy Barongs of the island of Bali, Indonesia, for instance, appear in ritual dramas, lumbering through the crowds, engaging audience members directly and inviting them to take an active part in the mythmaking. After villagers participate in Barong's fight against the forces of chaos in the performance, they are assured that calm has been restored and that all is right in the world.

King of the spirits and leader of the forces of good, Barong Ket is like an oversized village guardian for many residents of Bali. The best-known Barong performances involve his battles with the demon queen Rangda. When the witch Rangda creates chaos, the lionlike Barong Ket comes to the rescue, fighting off the villains with a ferocious display. In the battles, which are at once theater and ritual, neither side ever wins. Instead, the forces of order and chaos remain in balance.

But Barong Ket is also mischievous, often teasing and joking with village residents. Most villages in Bali have a Barong costume similar to the one shown above, and young men take theirs on the road to visit other Barongs as part of a seasonal celebration. These trips bring nearby communities together and allow the young men to meet women outside their village.

Different regions in Bali have different Barong costumes, each resembling a different animal. Barong Ket resembles a lion, Barong Bangkal a wild boar, Barong Machan a tiger, Barong Lembu a cow, and Barong Asu a dog. Barong Ket is the best-known kind of Barong because it is from the Gianyar region, where the tourist hub of Ubud is located.

These dramas came to the wide attention of Western audiences in the 1930s thanks to noted American Museum of Natural History anthropologist Margaret Mead and her colleague Gregory Bateson.

A BARONG FROM BALI (Opposite) This Barong Ket costume was commissioned by the American Museum of Natural History and made by the male members of Ubud village in Bali in 2011. Its design and construction was overseen by a prominent member of the community, Ni Wayan Murni. The materials are wood, water buffalo hide, synthetic hair, glass, feathers, palm fibers, metal, paint, gilding, textiles, and dye.

SHADOW PUPPETS (Right) These puppets of Rangda and Tanting Mas are from Bali, 1984. Rangda is the half-goddess, half-witch demon queen of Bali who often battles Barongs. Terrifying to behold, she is usually shown as a mostly nude old woman with long, unkempt hair, pendulous breasts, claws, fangs, and a long, protruding tongue. Tanting Mas is another queen of Balinese mythology, said to be angry and vengeful.

LIVE PERFORMANCE
A contemporary photo of a Barong performance in Bali. One dancer is responsible for moving the head and clacking the teeth, while a second dancer wiggles Barong's golden tail. Barong costumes may have been inspired by the elaborate costumes of the Chinese Lion and Unicorn Dances.

Greek Giants

Giant Facts

- Geological events tend to destroy the skulls of prehistoric elephant relatives, leaving only enormous, humanlike long bones, vertebrae, and ribs.

- The long bones of elephant relatives and humans are similar enough to be confused.

- Ancient authors often reported finding the remains of giants hundreds of feet tall—much taller than an elephant or any other animal. These reports may represent attempts to reconstruct the bones of several animals found jumbled together as a single giant.

From Paul Bunyan of American folklore to the Norse creator-god Ymir, humanlike giants populate the myths of many cultures. The ancient Greeks told stories of giants, describing them as flesh-and-blood creatures who lived and died—and whose bones could be found coming out of the ground where they were buried long ago. Indeed, even today large and surprisingly humanlike bones can be found in Greece. Modern scientists understand such bones to be the remains of mammoths, mastodons, and woolly rhinoceroses that once lived in the region. But ancient Greeks were largely unfamiliar with these massive animals, and many believed that the enormous bones they found were the remains of humanlike giants. Any nonhuman traits in the bones were thought to be due to the grotesque anatomical features of giants.

"Before there were any humans on Pallene, the story goes that a battle was fought between the gods and the giants. [Traces of the giants' demise] continue to be seen to this day, whenever torrents swell with rain and excessive water breaks their banks and floods the fields. They say that even now in gullies and ravines the people discover bones of immeasurable enormity, like men's carcasses but far bigger."

—Greek historian Solinus, ca. 200 CE

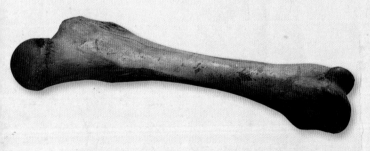

A GIANT'S LEG OR JUST A GIANT LEG? This enormous bone (*Mammuthus primigenius* femur, 500,000 to 10,000 years old) is from a woolly mammoth found in Alaska, but it looks very much like a human arm or leg bone, only much bigger. Many ancient Greeks thought the same thing, and when they found bones like these from other kinds of mammoths, they often interpreted them as the bones of giants.

THE BATTLE WITH THE GODS

ACCORDING TO GREEK MYTH, the giants were the children of Uranus (the Sky) and Gaia (the Earth), but were almost never born. Afraid the giants would be too powerful, Uranus would not allow them to be born, imprisoning them in Gaia's womb. Gaia convinced her youngest son, Kronos, to attack Uranus; he did and the blood that spilled on Gaia released the giants from their prison.

Kronos took power, but was soon overthrown by the god Zeus. The giants were enraged by the defeat of their savior and brother, and they took up trees as clubs and boulders as missiles, waging war on Zeus and the other Greek gods in an epic battle—the Gigantomachy. But the giants were ultimately defeated and buried under mountains, where their tormented shivers were said to cause earthquakes and volcanic eruptions.

GIGANTOMACHY An engraving depicting the epic Gigantomachy battle, by Dutch printmaker Nicolaes Cornelisz Witsen, 1659.

• The plural of Cyclops
is Cyclopes (pronounced
"sigh-KLO-peez").

• Cyclopes are
enormous, humanlike
creatures with a single
eye in the middle of
their foreheads.

• One group of Cyclopes
worked as blacksmiths
to the gods and were
praised for their fine
craftsmanship. Today,
well-constructed stone
walls are sometimes
called "cyclopean."

• Another group
of Cyclopes appear
in Homer's *Odyssey*.
Homer describes
them as grotesquely
ugly, ungainly, strong,
stubborn brutes who
are prone to aggression
and cannibalism.

CYCLOPES

The one-eyed giants of Greek myths called Cyclopes were usually said to live on the island of Sicily in the Mediterranean Sea. Significantly, the island was once home to ancient elephants whose enormous, fossilized skulls and bones can still be found today eroding out of cliffs and hillsides. As far back as the 1370s, scholars have suggested that when the first inhabitants of the island encountered elephant skulls, they might have mistaken the large central hole where the trunk was attached for the enormous single eye socket of a Cyclops.

POLYPHEMUS An early engraving, likely British, depicting the Cyclops Polyphemus attacking Odysseus's ships.

The Greek poet Homer describes an encounter between the hero Odysseus and a Cyclops named Polyphemus in his epic tale, *Odyssey*, which dates back to at least 800 BCE:

On his way home from the Trojan War, the brave adventurer Odysseus and his crew landed on the island of Sicily. Happy to find food in a cave, they gorged themselves until the cave's occupant, a ferocious Cyclops named Polyphemus, returned home and began to eat the men one by one. Polyphemus soon asked Odysseus his name and he replied, "My name is Nobody." That evening, Odysseus and his men planned their escape—first they drove a stake into Polyphemus's one eye. Screaming in pain, Polyphemus called to his brother Cyclopes, "Help! Nobody is hurting me!" Confused, they ignored the cries, and Polyphemus lost his only eye. In the morning, Polyphemus let his sheep out to graze after feeling along the animals' backs to make sure the men weren't riding on top. But Odysseus and his crew had tied themselves under the sheep's bellies, so they slipped by, unnoticed by the blinded Cyclops.

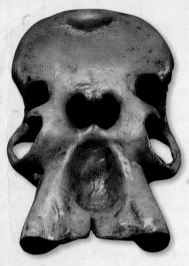

DWARF ELEPHANT SKULL The opening in the center of this cast of a dwarf elephant skull (*Elephas falconeri*) is where the animal's trunk attaches. (The original skull was found in Sicily, and is between 781,000 and 126,000 years old.) Ancient Greeks may have interpreted the large trunk opening as the massive, single eye socket of a Cyclops.

BESTIARY An illustration of fantastic creatures from *Cosmographia*, by Sebastian Münster, 1544; a female Cyclops is seen second from left.

A GIANT'S BRIDGE?

THE SPECTACULAR GIANT'S CAUSEWAY on the northeast coast of Ireland consists of about forty thousand interlocking columns of basalt rock. Formations like this one are typically the result of volcanic activity. Some sixty-five million years ago, lava flowed over the area. As the lava cooled, it contracted, fracturing into the columns seen today. According to Irish myth, the giant-hero Finn MacCool (also spelled Fionn mac Cumhaill) built the causeway so he could walk to Scotland to fight the Scottish giant Benandonner. Some scholars point to similarities in Irish myths such as this one and Greco-Roman myths.

GIANT STEPS A dramatic view of the Giant's Causeway in northeast Ireland.

SEEING IS BELIEVING

The people of Tingis (modern-day Tangier, Morocco) once boasted that their city's founder was a giant named Antaeus, shown here in an engraving for Dante's *Inferno* by nineteenth-century French artist Gustave Doré. Antaeus, they claimed, was buried in a mound south of town. To test the claim, Roman soldiers dug into the mound in 81 BCE. Much to their surprise, an enormous skeleton surfaced—which they then reburied with great honors. Modern scientists confirm that ancient elephant fossils are common in the area.

Chapter 4
UNICORNS, WEST & EAST

Alice could not help her lips curling up into
a smile as she began: "Do you know, I always
thought unicorns were fabulous monsters, too?
I never saw one alive before!"
"Well, now that we have seen each other,"
said the unicorn, "if you'll believe in me,
I'll believe in you."

—Lewis Carroll,
Through the Looking Glass (1871)

ARE ALL MYTHIC CREATURES SCARY? While many mythic creatures
are man-eating monsters or evil spirits, others, like unicorns, are powerful and
peaceful. Both the pearly white unicorn of European lore and the benevolent Asian
unicorn avoid contact with humans, preferring to remain unseen. When humans
do encounter unicorns, the creatures cause them no harm, a favor that is not always
returned. Indeed, countless stories tell of humans hunting European unicorns and
luring them into traps.

AMERICAN UNICORNS?
(Opposite) Detail of a
ca. 1575–1610 engraving
titled *America from the
Four Continents*, by Julius
Goltzius after Maerten de
Vos. Two unicorns pull a
chariot (not seen) carrying
a Native American figure
personifying America.

European Unicorns

- In most stories, they live deep in the forest and are rarely seen by people.

- White coat—but some early authors and artists described it as yellowish red or even brown.

- Usually a horse's body, often with cloven hooves or a beard like a goat; sometimes the entire body looks like a goat's.

- Long, white spiraled horn—but some early Greek naturalists described a shorter, blunter horn colored red or black.

- Tail of a lion—but some descriptions include the tail of a horse, goat, or boar.

AN ANCIENT TALE

You may have heard that the one-horned unicorn is so magical that its horn can counteract poisons, and it is so elusive that no person can catch it. But did you know these unicorn stories began in ancient Greece? Over two thousand years ago, Greek travelers told tales of unicorns living in far-off lands. As the fabulous accounts spread around the Western world, few people questioned that unicorns actually existed. Indeed, in about 300 BCE, scholars translating the Old Testament from

Of the UNICORN.

Hebrew into Greek concluded that the Hebrew term *re'em* referred to a unicorn (today some experts think it referred to a type of wild ox or an ancestor of cattle). Even early naturalists considered the unicorn to be a living animal. Several ancient catalogs of animals of the world include unicorns and describe them as solitary beasts that often battle lions and elephants.

NATURAL HISTORY BOOK (Above) In 1551, Swiss naturalist Konrad Gesner wrote *Historiae Animalium*, a book describing all of the animals that he thought lived on Earth, including a description and illustration of a unicorn, presumably based on the accounts of travelers to far-off lands. English writer Edward Topsell translated much of Gesner's work for use in his own book, *The History of Four-Footed Beasts*. This illustration is from the 1658 edition.

THE CHRISTIAN UNICORN (Opposite) Art historians have long considered the unicorn to be a symbol for Christ, a link seen most clearly in the story of a maiden capturing a unicorn. The unicorn's placing its head in the lap of the young maiden, or virgin, recalls baby Jesus lying in the lap of the Virgin Mary.

PURIFICATION (Above) In some Christian stories and artworks, the unicorn dips its horn into poisoned water to purify it for the other animals to drink, a reference to the story of Christ's sacrifice to cleanse the sins of mankind. This engraving, *The Unicorn Purifies the Water with His Horn*, is by Jean Duvet, ca. 1540–51.

ROYAL RESPECT (Right) Even today, unicorns remain objects of wonder and beauty, often appearing as characters in popular movies and books. But they can also symbolize majesty and power. Strong and powerful unicorns are featured in the royal arms of Scotland, shown here in an engraving from *Chambers's Encyclopaedia*, 1871.

PUREST CREATURE (Following pages) This engraving, *Triumph of the Unicorn*, by French artist Jean Duvet, 1540–50, depicts a procession headed by God the Father as Zeus who is welcoming the pure unicorn, symbolizing the son of God, into heaven.

Royal Arms of Scotland, previous to the Union.

UNICORN FOLKTALE

THE FOLLOWING STORY is adapted from medieval European folktales, but Greek authors told similar stories over two thousand years ago:

HUNT FOR THE UNICORN

Once upon a time, a hunter in the forest saw a brilliant white unicorn in the distance, emerging from a river and gleaming like the moon. Enchanted by the sight, the hunter called together his friends and gave chase. But the unicorn knew that men could never catch him, so he playfully waited for the hunters to draw close before bounding out of view.

UNICORN AND THE MAIDEN This hand-colored pen-and-ink drawing illustrating the "Hunt for the Unicorn" story is from an English illuminated manuscript of ca. 1250.

After a while, the unicorn came to a stop in front of a beautiful young maiden sitting under a tree. She reached out, combed his curling mane, and rubbed his horn until he lay his head in her lap. But it was a trap! Looking up at the maiden, the unicorn saw her brown eyes were filled with tears and realized her deceit too late—the dogs and men suddenly seized him and carried him away.

Afterward, the maiden remained in the woods, despondent. As she leaned down to wash away her tears in the stream, a movement in the distance caught her eye: she couldn't be sure, but she thought it was the shining horn of a unicorn disappearing into the night.

MAGICAL HORNS

Many stories of unicorns refer to the magical properties of their horns, a claim first made by a Greek physician named Ctesias nearly 2,400 years ago. Those lucky enough to possess a horn might take advantage of its healing properties, which ranged from detecting and neutralizing poisons and curing fevers to prolonging youth and acting as an aphrodisiac.

Before Europeans encountered what we know today are narwhal tusks—enormous "horns" that are the tusks of the male narwhal, a kind of Arctic whale—unicorns were often described as having horns

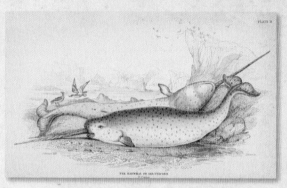

in a variety of sizes, shapes, and colors. But in the Middle Ages, Danish sailors and other merchants from the North brought narwhal tusks to European markets, where buyers considered them to be valuable, magical remains of elusive unicorns. From then on, nearly all descriptions of unicorn horns are consistent: they are long, white, and spiraled, just like the narwhal tusk.

IS THIS A UNICORN? (Above) An illustration of male narwhals from *The Naturalist's Library*, by Scottish naturalist and aristocrat Sir William Jardine, 1846.

HOLY HORN (Left) The monastery of Saint Mary in Guadalupe, Spain, gave this African white rhinoceros horn (near left) to Pope Gregory XIV as he lay dying in 1590. Like unicorn horns, rhinoceros horns were thought to have magical, curative properties. Although the tip of the horn was cut off and administered to the Pope, it proved ineffective and he died shortly thereafter. The decorative case is shown at far left.

"[There are] wild elephants and plenty of unicorns, which are scarcely smaller than elephants. They have the hair of a buffalo and feet like an elephant's. They have a single large, black horn in the middle of the forehead. . . . They have a head like a wild boar's and always carry it stooped toward the ground. They spend their time by preference wallowing in mud and slime. They are very ugly brutes to look at. They are not at all such as we describe them when we relate that they let themselves be captured by virgins."

—Italian explorer Marco Polo, ca. 1300, most likely describing a Sumatran rhinoceros

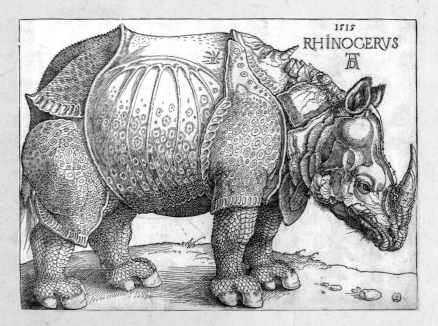

UNICORN SIGN (Above)
This sign was made around 1750 and hung above the door to a German apothecary, or pharmacy, and shows a continuation of the medieval association of unicorns and medicine. Indeed, in medieval Europe, unicorn horns were thought to be able to cure a range of illnesses, from epilepsy to the plague. This unicorn's horn is actually a narwhal tusk.

"UGLY BRUTES" (Left)
Woodcut engraving of a Sumatran rhinoceros by Albrecht Dürer, 1515.

Asian Unicorns

Long before the pearly white unicorn of European lore, a one-horned, magical animal was said to roam the Eastern world—Asia's version of the unicorn. First mentioned in written stories around 2700 BCE, this unicorn is described as a creature of great power and wisdom. Always benevolent, it avoids fighting at all costs and walks so softly it will not crush a blade of grass. Much like its European cousin, the Asian unicorn enjoys its solitude and cannot be captured. Its rare appearances are omens, celebrating just and wise rulers. Asian unicorns bore different names in different countries, although they were similar creatures; in Japan the unicorn was called a *kirin*, and in China it was known as a *qilin*.

KIRIN NETSUKE (Above) This netsuke, a toggle or fastener used to attach containers to clothing, is carved in the shape of a Japanese unicorn, called a *kirin*. It is from nineteenth-century Japan, and made of ivory, wood, glass, and pigment.

CHINESE UNICORN (Left) Detail from a porcelain charger from China decorated with a Chinese unicorn, called a *qilin*, ca. 1350.

"*Thousands of years ago, the sage Fu Hsi was sitting by a river when he was splashed with water. Raising his eyes, he saw the unicorn, which the Chinese call the qilin ('chee-lin'), wading carefully through the river. The animal resembled a deer but had shining scales like a dragon. A single horn grew from its forehead. Its back was covered with strange signs and magic symbols. As the qilin walked away, Fu Hsi grabbed a stick and traced the symbols as best he could in the dirt. These drawings were the qilin's gift to China—from them would evolve the characters of the first written language.*"

—Adapted from ancient
Chinese stories

INCENSE BURNER (Above) This copper-alloy incense burner from the Ming dynasty (ca. 1368–1644) is in the form of a Chinese unicorn, or *qilin*. To some Chinese, burning incense helps establish a connection between our world and the world of gods and ancestors.

CARVED MASK (Left) This nineteenth-century painted Japanese kirin mask, made of wood and lacquer, has a hinged jaw and was likely used in festivals.

Chapter 5
MODERN MYTHS— EARTH CREATURES

In the [Tian Shan] mountains themselves live a wild people,
who have nothing in common with other human beings,
a pelt covers the entire body of these creatures. . . . They run
around in the hills like animals and eat foliage and grass
and whatever else they can find.

—German traveler Johann Schiltberger, ca. 1400

ARE MYTHIC CREATURES ALL RELICS OF THE PAST? Of course not. Around the world today, people tell stories about creatures like bigfoot and the Himalayan yeti. The terrifying chupacabra is a modern myth very much alive in the Americas. Thanks largely to television and the Internet, stories about the chupacabra and other modern mythic creatures spread quickly between communities, countries, and even continents. And as mythic creatures take root in new settings, they often change to suit their new audiences. In some places, the chupacabra is a mysterious predator lurking in the forest; in others, it is a sensational, sometimes tongue-in-cheek, media creation.

BIGFOOT The modern legend of the giant mythic half-man half-ape figure known as bigfoot has become part of popular culture. Here, a staged photograph of what bigfoot might look like if one encountered it in the forest.

Chupacabra

Chupacabra Facts

• Chupacabras are fierce, but not terribly big. Most witnesses say they are no larger than an average-sized dog.

• Descriptions vary widely, but most chupacabras have red eyes and large fangs.

• Some witnesses say that the chupacabra walks on two legs and supposedly hops like a kangaroo, but others say it walks on four.

• Some depictions show it with lizardlike skin, while others show it with fur.

• Chupacabras have pronounced backbones, which are sometimes covered with sharp spines.

People tell of the chupacabra's glowing red eyes and glistening fangs, and of how the beast lurks in the forest, preying on goats and cattle, terrifying local residents. Chupacabra means "goat sucker" in Spanish, and according to reports, the creature acts much like a vampire, killing animals by sucking their blood. Some witnesses even report finding animal bodies that look like they were cut open with a knife. As it turns out, however, these events aren't necessarily so strange. Disease and infection can kill seemingly healthy animals, and some insects drink blood from fresh corpses. When animals die, gases in their bodies can expand, splitting them open with seemingly surgical precision.

Although similar stories date back several decades, the first major wave of alleged chupacabra sightings came from farmers in Puerto Rico in the late 1980s and early 1990s. Today people across much of Latin America and the southwestern United States tell tales of the chupacabra. The fanged creature can also be spotted on T-shirts, coffee mugs, and other souvenir items, and even in art galleries and toy stores.

MODERN MONSTER (Right) A contemporary artist's interpretation of the fearsome chupacabra, lying in wait for its next victim.

CARVED FIGURINE (Opposite) This colorful wooden chupacabra carving, ca. 2007, is an *alebrije*—a brightly painted Mexican sculpture of a fantastical creature. Artists in Oaxaca, Mexico, have been making such sculptures of imagined animals for decades. Here, the artist, T. Viguera, has applied the traditional *alebrije* style to the mythic chupacabra creature from popular culture.

Beyond Bigfoot

Primates, from tiny monkeys to larger chimpanzees and gorillas, fascinate us, maybe because we see in them so much of ourselves. Primates are intelligent and often take care of one another, especially their young. But they can also be violent, attacking outsiders and even turning on friends and family. So perhaps it's not surprising that many people around the world tell stories of creatures that appear

MYSTERIOUS APE-MEN AROUND THE WORLD

HIBAGON According to Japanese legends, the *hibagon* stands only five feet tall, shorter than most other bigfoot-like creatures. But its footprints are enormous—two or three times the size of a human's.

ALMAS Hair-covered wild men who supposedly live in the mountains of central Asia and Mongolia.

YETI Westerners often call the yeti the "abominable snowman" of Tibet.

WILD MEN OF BORNEO Reports of the "wild men of Borneo" probably referred to large, hairy primates called orangutans. In Indonesian, *orang hutan* means "man of the forest."

CHEMOSIT Some witnesses say that the *chemosit* looks like a hyena or a bear and call it a Nandi bear, after a Kenyan tribe who lives in its reported range. The Nandi people, however, consider the creature to be an enormous, ferocious primate that enjoys eating the brains of its victims.

ORANG PENDEK *Orang pendek* means "short person" in Indonesian, an appropriate name considering its supposedly short stature and humanlike face. Local folklore holds that the elusive creatures have backward-pointing feet to confuse anyone trying to track them.

YOWIE Over three thousand distinct *yowie* sightings have been reported in the Blue Mountain area west of Sydney in the past few decades.

to be half-human and half-ape. They are typically described as large, hairy creatures that walk on two legs but always seem to stay just out of sight. These mythic primates, like bigfoot, yeti, or even King Kong, are sometimes gentle, sometimes ferocious. Not quite human, not quite beast, these creatures hint at our other side.

BIGFOOT (SASQUATCH) The majority of bigfoot sightings occur in the northwestern United States and Canada, but reports of the creature have come from all across North America.

YEREN According to Chinese legend, when the *yeren* encounters a human, it grabs him or her tightly by the arms and faints, overwhelmed with joy. When it awakes, still holding on, it eats its victim.

SKUNK APES Some Floridians report that terrible-smelling "skunk apes" inhabit Everglades National Park.

MAPINGUARI In 1937, a *mapinguari* reportedly went on a three-week rampage in central Brazil. Witnesses report that over one hundred cows were found slaughtered, each with its massive tongue ripped from its body.

GIGANTOPITHECUS

Enormous apes aren't only creatures of myth: the massive creature shown on the opposite page is a reconstruction of an extinct primate called *Gigantopithecus blacki*. A very distant relative of humans, this animal lived in Southeast Asia for almost a million years, until about three hundred thousand years ago. And it is possible that small groups of these apes survived even longer. If so, early humans in the area could have encountered the creatures. More recently, people in China have collected the fossilized teeth and jaws of *Gigantopithecus* for their alleged healing powers. Anyone who discovered such a large jaw could have easily imagined that it came from an ape so colossal that it would dwarf a human.

The human imagination shapes mythic creatures—and can color our view of biological ones. When

Western explorers in Africa first encountered gorillas, they were terrified, describing these typically reclusive animals as aggressive and violent. In 1847, Thomas S. Savage, an American missionary in Gabon, Africa, wrote:

> When the male [gorilla] is first seen he gives a terrific yell, that resonates far and wide through the forest. His underlip hangs over the chin, and his hairy ridge and scalp are contracted upon the brow, presenting an aspect of indescribable ferocity. He then approaches the hunter in great fury, pouring out his horrid cries in quick succession. The hunter waits until the animal grasps the barrel of his gun, and as he carries it to his mouth, he fires. Should the gun fail to go off, the barrel is crushed between the teeth, and the encounter soon proves fatal to the hunter.

APE ASSEMBLY

(Opposite) This cast of a lower jawbone discovered in the autonomous region of Guangxi, China, is from the extinct ape *Gigantopithecus blacki*. Few other fossils of this creature have ever been found. Nonetheless, scientists at the American Museum of Natural History have managed to learn a considerable amount from the fragmentary evidence available. Experts turned to gorillas, the largest living apes, as models and observed a strong relationship between jaw and limb size for these massive, mostly ground-dwelling apes. Then, by applying that gorilla model to this *Gigantopithecus* jaw, they determined the approximate size of the creature shown in the picture. By their estimate, this individual weighed almost 800 pounds (360 kilograms).

GIGANTOPITHECUS BLACKI

(Right) This is a reconstruction of the enormous ape called *Gigantopithecus blacki*. We don't know if humans ever saw one alive—the creature probably went extinct about three hundred thousand years ago. But fossilized jaws and teeth from this primate may have inspired stories of large humanlike creatures in the parts of Asia where the remains were found.

PART 3

AIR

Creatures of the Sky

Have you ever wondered what it feels like to fly? The smallest bird has powers we will never share. But mythic creatures of the air have even greater powers. Imagine a bird so large it blocks out the sky or stirs up storms with its wings. In myths and legends, winged horses, lions, and even people all have the power of flight. These stories help express the wonder and awe inspired by looking up at the sky.

DIVINE HORSE Pegasus depicted in a delicate engraving, ca. 1509–16, by Italian printmaker Jacopo de' Barbari.

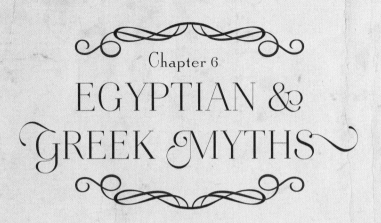

Chapter 6
EGYPTIAN & GREEK MYTHS

Hail, children of Zeus! Grant lovely song and celebrate the holy race of the deathless gods who are forever, those that were born of Earth and starry Heaven and gloomy Night and them that briny Sea did rear. Tell how at the first gods and earth came to be, and rivers, and the boundless sea with its raging swell, and the gleaming stars, and the wide heaven above.

—Hesiod, *Theogony*, ca. 700 BCE

HOW OLD ARE GREEK MYTHS? Zeus and many other Greek gods who dwelled on Mount Olympus—from Aphrodite to Poseidon—are familiar to many readers. The Greek stories of gods, heroes, and monsters have been told and retold around the world, and are still told today. The earliest known versions of these myths date back more than 2,700 years, appearing in written form in the works of the Greek poets Homer and Hesiod. But some of the myths are much older. Many of the stories we think of as Greek myths have roots in other, more ancient, cultures, such as Egyptian and Sumerian.

GREEK MYTH (Opposite) In one of the most famous Greek myths, Perseus, son of Zeus and a mortal princess, Danaë, rides the winged horse Pegasus to Aethiopia to kill the sea monster threatening the princess Andromeda. This engraving by printmaker Pieter Nolpe is dated 1642.

Sphinx

At least 4,500 years ago—more than 2,000 years before Sophocles wrote of the Sphinx—Egyptian artists carved half-human, half-lion statues out of stone. And some 3,500 years ago, artists in Mesopotamia depicted similar creatures and may have transmitted the image to Greece.

The Great Sphinx of Giza has stood guard in front of the pyramids since around 2500 BCE. Unlike the half-lion, half-woman Sphinx of Greek myth, the Great Sphinx combines the body of a lion with the head of a man—King Khafre, the ruler of Egypt at that time. Other Egyptian sphinxes, however, have the heads of rams or falcons. And while the Sphinx of Greek myth is cruel and aggressive, Egyptian sphinxes are considered benign symbols of powerful rulers.

GREEK SPHINX (Above) The Sphinx decorates a terracotta black-figure lekythos (oil container) from Greece, ca. 500 BCE.

GREAT SPHINX (Right) Photograph, ca. 1867–99, of the Great Sphinx of Giza, the world's largest monolith at 240 feet (73 meters) long and 66 feet (20 meters) high. The pyramids of Khafre (right) and Menkaure (left) are visible behind the Sphinx.

THE STORY OF THE SPHINX

MANY YEARS AGO, THE SPHINX sat in front of the gates to the ancient Greek city of Thebes. The Sphinx was a terrible monster with a lion's body and a woman's head—and a fondness for riddles. She asked a question of everyone who passed, eating anyone who couldn't answer. "What has one voice and walks on four legs in the morning, two legs at noon, and three legs in the evening?" No one had ever answered correctly, and the Sphinx was well fed.

But one day a clever man named Oedipus came along and gave the correct answer, "man." A person crawls on all fours as a baby, walks on two legs as an adult, and uses a cane—a third leg—in old age. Distraught over being outwitted, the Sphinx threw herself off her high perch and died on the road below.

—Adapted from *Oedipus Rex*
by the Greek playwright
Sophocles (ca. 495–406 BCE)

ATHANASII KIRCHERI E SOCIETATE IESV
OEDIPVS ÆGYPTIACVS
AD FERDINANDVM III CÆSAREM SEMPER AVGVSTVM.

THE RIDDLE
Frontispiece of *Oedipus Aegyptiacus*, 1652, a work of Egyptology written by seventeenth-century German Jesuit scholar Athanasius Kircher. It depicts Oedipus solving the Sphinx's riddle.

Pegasus

Pegasus Facts

- Divine white horse with wings.

- Pegasus was the son of the monster Medusa (he sprung from her blood) and Poseidon, the god of the seas and of horses.

- Pegasus was kind, helpful, and brave. The constellation named after him even shares a star with the constellation of Andromeda, a maiden he helped save.

- Pegasus allowed only two mortals to ride him: the heroes Perseus and Bellerophon.

The white, winged horse Pegasus is only a minor character in Greek myths, serving as the loyal steed and companion to the heroes Perseus and Bellerophon as they battle with monsters. Although Pegasus doesn't show up in many myths, he was a favorite subject of Greek artists. Even today, Pegasus is among the most popular images from Greek myth, appearing on everything from corporate logos to figures on carousels. Indeed, Pegasus is so well known that today any winged horse is called a pegasus.

SILVER COIN Stories of Pegasus were particularly popular in the ancient city of Corinth, Greece, which is where this coin is from (584–550 BCE). The winged horse was used as the city's emblem and appeared on coins of the city for hundreds of years.

NEW WORLD PEGASUS A pegasus is featured in this detail from a late-nineteenth-century fresco by Edward J. Holslag on the ceiling of the Library of Congress's Thomas Jefferson building in Washington, D.C.

CARVED PEGASUS
This carved wooden Pegasus figure, made by American artist Joe Leonard in 1996 for a private collector, is styled after the animals found on carousels. This statue's wings, however, would make it impossible for anyone to sit on the creature's back.

LOYAL COMPANION

LONG AGO, THE YOUNG Greek hero Perseus set out on a seemingly impossible quest: to slay the hideous Medusa. With a head covered in snakes instead of hair, Medusa was so ugly that anyone who looked at her turned to stone. For many days, Perseus traveled in search of Medusa. Finally, he found her and her two sisters resting among the statues of other heroes, all turned to stone by Medusa's gaze. But Perseus had consulted the gods and knew how to defeat the monster. Looking only at Medusa's reflection in a polished shield, Perseus chopped off her horrible head with a sickle. The winged horse Pegasus sprang from Medusa's neck. Medusa's two sisters were furious and chased after Perseus. But Pegasus allowed the hero to climb on his back, and the two flew away to safety.

—Adapted from ancient Greek myths

PERSEUS BEHEADING MEDUSA An engraving by Dutch printmaker Abraham de Bruyn, 1584, depicts the birth of Pegasus from the bloody neck of Medusa.

"A long time ago, the Greek hero Bellerophon set out to kill the fire-breathing Chimera, a beast with a lion's head, a goat's body, and a serpent's tail. The goddess Athena helped Bellerophon tame Pegasus, and with the winged horse's aid, Bellerophon killed the monster. After this glorious victory, Bellerophon thought himself the equal of the gods and urged Pegasus to fly him to Mount Olympus. But Bellerophon's arrogance enraged the gods. Zeus sent a fly to bite Pegasus, causing him to rear back and sending Bellerophon hurtling to the ground. He then spent the rest of his days wandering as an outcast. Pegasus remained at Olympus for the rest of his life, carrying Zeus's lightning bolts on his back. When Pegasus died, Zeus transformed him into a constellation, which can be seen to this day."

—Adapted from Homer's *Iliad*, ca. 800–600 BCE,
and other ancient Greek myths

KYLIX (Left) Bellerophon slays the Chimera (the creature at right) as Pegasus (at left) rears overhead on this black-figure terracotta Greek kylix (wine cup), ca. 570–550 BCE. In some portrayals, the goat's torso and head rise out of the middle of the Chimera's body, as seen here.

HERO QUEST (Following pages) Bellerophon and the Chimera, in a detail from *The Power of Eloquence*, ca. 1724, a ceiling fresco at the Palazzo Sandi-Porto (now Cipollato), Venice, Italy, by Giovanni Battista Tiepolo.

Chapter 7
STRIKE FROM THE SKY

It was for all the world like an eagle, but one indeed of
enormous size; so big in fact that its wings covered an extent
of 30 paces. . . . And it is so strong that it will seize an elephant
in its talons and carry him high into the air, and drop him so that
he is smashed to pieces. . . . The people of those isles call this bird
a Ruc, and it has no other name.

—Rustichello da Pisa, *The Travels of Marco Polo*,
Sir Henry Yule (translator), 1875

WHAT IF BIRDS GREW TO ENORMOUS SIZES? Many stories tell of giant
birds that swoop down from the sky to seize animals—sometimes even humans.
Such stories are not entirely legend. Living birds such as eagles, hawks, and falcons
dart down to snatch snakes, fish, rabbits, and other animals. Fossils show that
thousands of years ago, large birds preyed on people, and in some remote areas, they
remain a threat to small children. Many mythic creatures have supernatural powers,
or combine features of different animals into one. But all it really takes to turn a
bird into a mythic monster is to make it larger.

COLOSSAL BIRD
(Opposite) A shipwrecked
traveler, likely Sinbad,
clinging to the legs of a
giant Roc. Illustration from
Marvels of Creation, by
Persian cosmographer
Zakariya al-Qazwini
(ca. 1203–83).

Roc

Roc Facts

- Looks like a giant eagle.

- Eats elephants and snakes.

- Likely based on the *Aepyornis*, an extinct bird of Madagascar.

- In *The Arabian Nights*, Sinbad finds a white dome-shaped building with no doors—the dome is a Roc's egg, and the entire island its nest.

- Legs as thick as tree trunks; trapped in the Roc's island nest, Sinbad ties himself to the Roc's leg to escape.

MYTHIC ROC (Right) The ancient story of Sinbad the Sailor, told in *The Arabian Nights*, describes a giant mythic bird, bigger than any bird that has ever lived. In such stories, the Roc is so large it can carry off elephants, but no living bird could actually carry such a heavy load. Here, a model of the giant bird of myth.

One of the greatest explorers of all time was the Moroccan-born Islamic scholar and judge Ibn Battuta (1304–ca. 1368), who in the 1300s journeyed 73,000 miles (117,000 kilometers) across the Islamic world—about three times as far as the more famous Italian explorer Marco Polo (ca. 1254–1324). Ibn Battuta dictated his memoir, *Rihla*, which recounts his amazing journeys.

Thirteenth-century Italian writer Rustichello da Pisa, the coauthor of *The Travels of Marco Polo*, recounts in that book Ibn Battuta's description of what looked like a mountain floating in midair above the China Sea:

> The sailors were weeping and bidding each other adieu, so I called out, "What is the matter?" They replied, "What we took for a mountain is the Rukh. If it sees us, it will send us to destruction." . . . A fair wind . . . turned us from the direction in which the Rukh was; so we did not see him well enough to take cognizance of his real shape.

In fact, a giant bird of the *Aepyornis* genus once lived on the island of Madagascar, off the southeast coast of Africa in the Indian Ocean (see pages 104–5). Yet the Roc is more than a misidentified *Aepyornis*. Stories of the Roc are based on Garuda, a birdlike creature found in Hindu stories dating back thousands of years, in which Garuda preys on giant snakes and elephants (see pages 106–15). The Roc is also said to eat both snakes and elephants, suggesting that the stories share a common origin.

A ROC'S FEATHER? (Above) Marco Polo, who introduced many previously unknown wonders of Asia to Europeans, wrote that the Mongol emperor Kublai Khan was said to own a giant Roc feather: "They brought (as I heard) to the Great Kaan a feather of the said Ruc . . . a marvelous object! The Great Kaan was delighted with it, and gave great presents to those who brought it." Marco Polo's nineteenth-century translator, Sir Henry Yule, later suggested that the Great Khan was conned by a frond from a raffia palm tree, shown here.

ROCS WITH ROCKS (Right) In *The Arabian Nights*, a classic collection of stories from the Middle East, Sinbad's shipmates discover an immense Roc's egg, with a young Roc just emerging. They kill the young Roc and eat it, but soon find themselves attacked by its furious parents. They flee in their ship, but the angry Rocs follow, carrying massive boulders that they drop on the ship, smashing it to splinters. This drawing is from 1898, by English illustrator Henry J. Ford.

AEPYORNIS

Seven hundred years ago, Arab traders told of a bird so huge it could lift elephants into the sky. Sailors said it lived on an island off the southern coast of Africa. In fact, this island, Madagascar, was once home to the giant *Aepyornis*. Although it is now extinct, the *Aepyornis* was the largest bird that ever lived. It was called the elephant bird—even though it couldn't really lift an elephant. In fact, it couldn't even fly. But its large eggs helped fuel the legend of the mythical Roc.

ELEPHANT BIRD (Right) The two great explorers Marco Polo and Ibn Battuta both wrote that the legendary Roc lived near Madagascar. Bones and eggs have since proved that the half-ton *Aepyornis* really did live on the island. The nickname "elephant bird" also probably comes from the Roc story. *Aepyornis* could not have hunted elephants because it was too small—and because no elephants ever lived on Madagascar.

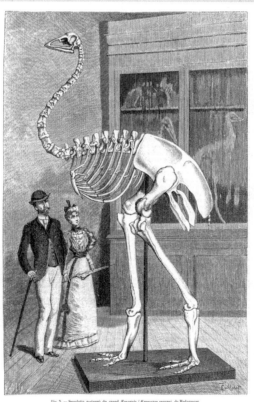

Fig. 5. — Squelette restauré du grand Æpyornis (*Æpyornis ingens*), de Madagascar.

AN ENORMOUS EGG (Below) *Aepyornis* eggs, the largest known bird egg, were found on the island of Madagascar in the nineteenth century. In 1864, W. Winwood Reade wrote, "The existence of the Roc of Marco Polo and *The Arabian Nights* is now proved by the discovery of an immense egg in a semi-fossil state in Madagascar." A member of the Antandroy people in Madagascar holds a fossilized *Aepyornis* egg in this recent photograph by Frans Lanting.

AN EXTINCT EAGLE
(Above) *Aepyornis* isn't the only giant bird to give rise to legends. The Maori people have long told of the *poukai*, a giant eagle that once lived in New Zealand. Evidence such as bones and talons have proved that the giant bird, now called Haast's Eagle (*Harpagornis moorei*), was more than a myth. And unlike *Aepyornis*, it could fly. It had a wingspan of nearly 10 feet (3 meters) and preyed on moas, large flightless birds related to ostriches. Haast's Eagle lived until about 1500 CE—recent enough to possibly have been encountered by Maori ancestors. Shown here is an actual-size reproduction of the talon of a Haast's Eagle.

THE LARGEST BIRD THAT EVER LIVED (Left) A life-size model of the *Aepyornis*; it would have towered over an average-sized adult.

Opposites Attack

Some mythic creatures fly solo. Others come in pairs. Sometimes, two characters are constantly at war with each other. These battling duos can help storytellers express abstract ideas. For instance, a saint slaying a dragon might symbolize the struggle between good and evil. But interpreting a story is rarely that simple. The same story may have many meanings and be told many different ways. In Asian stories, the giant, birdlike creature Garuda constantly attacks snakelike creatures known as Nagas. But this is no simple tale of good versus evil. Garuda and Nagas are identified with many pairs of opposites, including light and dark, the sun and moon, upper and lower, air and water, and Buddhism and other religions.

GARUDA

According to Hindu and Buddhist stories, Garuda spends an eternity hunting and killing Nagas. The feud started when a deity, Kasyapa, marries two sisters, Vinata and Kadru. Kasyapa gives each wife one wish. Kadru asks for a thousand children, and gives birth to a thousand snakes, the Nagas. Vinata wishes for just two children who would be superior to all of the Nagas. She bears Aruna, who becomes the charioteer of the sun god, and Garuda, who becomes the mount of Vishnu. The two sisters' rivalry continues until Vinata loses a bet and becomes the servant and prisoner of Kadru. Garuda is able to free his mother by stealing the nectar of immortality from the gods as a ransom, but he swears vengeance for his mother's maltreatment and has been fighting Nagas ever since.

Garuda Facts

• In Hinduism, Garuda is a single character, but in Buddhist stories, there are many Garudas.

• Human torso and arms; some Hindu representations of Garuda have four arms, while Buddhist Garudas sometimes have only wings.

• Wings, legs, tail, and the clawed feet of a bird.

• Head of a bird, or human head with beak.

• Garuda carries the Hindu god Vishnu on its back.

• Wings so large that they darken the sky; flapping wings can cause hurricanes.

• Garuda constantly battles the snakelike Nagas, and in some stories it wears defeated Nagas as jewelry.

• Garuda can protect people against snakes and snakebites, as well as poisons.

GARUDA CATCHING A NAGA (Opposite) This nineteenth-century Tibetan statuette made of gilded copper alloy shows Garuda attacking a Naga. The same story is told in many different art forms, styles, and materials throughout Asia.

The Hindu tradition has a wealth of stories and texts, including versions of the Garuda story dating back more than three thousand years. When Buddhism branched off from Hinduism around 500 BCE, these stories transformed as they spread throughout Asia and beyond. Today a billion people practice Hinduism, mostly in India, and another 350 million practice Buddhism. Garudas and Nagas can now be found in Balinese paintings, Himalayan bronzes, Japanese and Tibetan ritual dramas, Thai shadow puppets, and Cambodian architecture, as well as in countless local shrines in India and elsewhere.

In Hinduism, Garuda is a single character, but in Buddhist stories there are many Garudas. The Hindu Garuda carries the god Vishnu on his back, while in the Buddhist world Garuda is an agent of the faith, wrestling with Nagas until

they become Buddhist. Meanings can vary as much as details. For Buddhists, the story of Garuda overcoming Nagas symbolizes the spread of Buddhism throughout Asia, with Nagas representing indigenous religions and deities that were converted to Buddhism.

Today, Garuda is part of daily life in Asia. In addition to being evoked in worship, theater, art, and story, Garuda is the national symbol of Thailand and Indonesia. Garuda has also inspired the name of an airline (the national airline of Indonesia); a yoga pose; and characters in video games, comic books, television series, and card games.

GARUDA CARRYING VISHNU This ca. 1800 watercolor from India shows the god Vishnu and his consort Lakshmi riding on Garuda. In the Hindu tradition, Vishnu was the only god powerful enough to subdue Garuda. Garuda became Vishnu's mount, and the pair are often shown together in Hindu art.

READY TO STRIKE (Right) This stone Garuda statue in Indonesia, date unknown, has a human torso, a bird's head, and enormous wings and tail.

GARUDA SHADOW PUPPET (Below) Stories about Garuda and Nagas are told in many forms, including ritual drama. In performance, the Garuda is held in the puppeteer's right hand, above the Naga, which is held lower and in the left hand. This Balinese puppet from the 1930s, made of hide, wood, paint, and plant fiber, was collected by renowned American anthropologist Margaret Mead (1901–78).

GARUDA DANCE This Garuda bird dancer is performing at a Buddhist New Year's dance, January 1969, in Sikkim, India, in the Himalayas. Photograph by author and photographer Dr. Alice S. Kandell.

- *Naga* is the Sanskrit word for "snake," particularly the cobra.

- Nagas have split tongues caused by licking the grass on which Garuda spilled the nectar of eternal life.

- Human faces with cobralike hood; snake body and tail.

- Nagas live underground in caves, sometimes in jeweled palaces.

- The Naga king supports the world; when he moves it causes earthquakes.

- The Naga king has a thousand heads, which in Buddhism serve as an umbrella for the sleeping Buddha.

NAGAS

The snakelike Nagas are not always figures of evil like the Judeo-Christian serpents of the Old and New Testaments. Although some stories describe Nagas as Garuda's enemies, whom he perpetually punishes, Nagas are also worshiped in their own right. In Cambodia, for instance, Nagas are revered as the ancestors of the Cambodian people and the protectors of the Buddha. In other Buddhist societies, Nagas were sometimes assimilated with local deities. In Tibet, for example, Nagas are associated with the water serpent spirits called *klu*. In South India, Nagas are believed to aid in fertility, and women seek their help in having children.

NAGA DESCENDANT (Right) A cobra, one of the most revered creatures in Hindu culture.

NAGA KING (Opposite) A stone sculpture of the Naga king at Angkor Wat, the vast twelfth-century temple complex in northwest Cambodia.

NAGA THRONE In this nineteenth-century print from Bombay, the many-headed Naga king forms a throne for Narayana, an avatar of Vishnu, who is surrounded by other Hindu deities including his consort Lakshmi, with her hand on his legs, and the winged Garuda, to his far left.

BIRD VERSUS SNAKE (Left) Birds that attack snakes are common in stories around the world, including Greece, India, Iran, China, and Mexico. This Mexican stamp shows an eagle clutching a snake as a symbol of the founding of the Aztec civilization.

NAGA SHADOW PUPPET (Below left) Nagas, Garuda's traditional foes, can be portrayed in a variety of forms. This 1930s shadow puppet from Bali, Indonesia, shows a Naga as a winged serpent. It is made of hide, wood, paint, and plant fiber, and was collected by Margaret Mead.

NAGA SHRINE (Below) In South India, a cobra nest may become a shrine to the mythical Nagas, such as this one in Goa. Women offer the snakes milk, fruit, and flowers, and entice them out with songs and incense. People sometimes come within inches of deadly cobras without being injured.

Chapter 8
HEAVEN SENT

Half buried to her flaming breast
In this bright tree, she makes her nest,
Hundred-sunned Phoenix! when she must
Crumble at length to hoary dust;
Her gorgeous death-bed! her rich pyre
Burnt up with aromatic fire!
Her urn, sight high from spoiler men!
Her birthplace when self-born again!

—George Darley, from *Nepenthe*, 1839

A BIRD FROM ANOTHER WORLD? Divine birds appear in legends of Asia, Europe, and the Middle East—from China and Japan to ancient Greece, Rome, Egypt, and beyond. These creatures are said to come from a sacred realm and rarely visit the earth. When they do, they may be seen as a sign that a new era has begun or that a wise leader has taken the throne. Often linked with fire and the sun, these immortal birds bring messages of peace, renewal, and good fortune.

FABLE OF THE PHOENIX
(Opposite) This engraving of the legendary Greco-Roman phoenix rising from the ashes of its demise is by Aegidius Sadeler after Marcus Gheeraerts, 1608.

ASIAN PHOENIX

In Asia, the magical phoenix is said to reign over all the birds. Living only on spring water and bamboo seeds, this gentle ruler harms nothing—not even a blade of grass. In Chinese tradition, the phoenix, or *fenghuang*, appears only at times of peace, or to announce the birth of a virtuous emperor. Tales of birds much like the Asian phoenix are told in many regions of the world. These legends have sometimes changed as cultures have come together through travel, trade, and war, expanding and enriching each other.

ROOF CHARM Rows of ceramic mythic beasts guard the roof tiles of many palaces and temples in China. In a typical roof decoration of the imperial court, they are led by a divine figure riding a phoenix, much like the one shown here, ca. 1900.

春月堂
政子

をとめすのる
の代はめてく

鳥

KING OF BIRDS (Above) Detail of a Japanese phoenix with its brilliant plumage from a woodcut, ca. 1822, by famed Japanese artist Totoya Hokkei.

SWORD GUARD (Right) According to Asian legend, when a phoenix flies from heaven to earth, it likes to perch on a branch of a paulownia, or princess tree. Both the bird and the tree have been used as emblems of the Japanese empire. Here a golden phoenix hovers above paulownia blossoms on a Japanese sword guard, 1600–1850 (Edo period), a decorative art form inspired by Samurai armor.

SILK PHOENIXES

THERE WAS ONCE a girl named Saijosen who made the most beautiful embroidery in Japan. She stitched pictures of men, gods, and animals so artfully, it was as if living creatures were trapped in the silk.

One day as she sat working, an elderly man appeared beside her. "Stitch two phoenixes here," he said, pointing to a space on her embroidery. Saijosen was surprised at this request, but she did as she was told. Her visitor watched as she worked the whole day.

No sooner were the birds complete than their wings trembled and they rose from the cloth. The old man climbed on the back of one phoenix and motioned Saijosen to mount the other one. Then the two soared away to the land of the immortals, never to be seen again.

—Adapted from a Japanese folktale

KIMONO A close-up of a woman's formal kimono with phoenix detail, ca. 1920.

TILE (Above) In ancient Persian stories, a magical bird called the *simurgh* offers wisdom and kindness to people. Early pictures show the simurgh as a griffinlike beast with the wings of an eagle, tail of a peacock, head of a dog, and claws of a lion. But after Persia fell to the Mongols, this legendary bird began to look like the Chinese phoenix. It is difficult to say which bird the artist had in mind when designing the image on this tile from ca. 1250–1325.

EMBROIDERED SILK (Right) In Chinese tradition, the phoenix is the divine ruler of birds and a symbol of feminine grace. In these two silk panels from the 1800s (detail), made to be sewn on the sleeves of a woman's robe, white phoenixes float among cranes and peacocks. Richly embroidered panels like these were often saved after a garment became worn so they could be reused again and again.

Egyptian/Western Phoenix Facts

- A symbol of the sun, rebirth, renewal, resurrection, immortality.

- Lives for hundreds of years, dies, and is reborn from its ashes.

- Sometimes depicted with a nimbus of rays, like the sun.

- Size descriptions range from eagle- to ostrich-sized.

Egyptian/Western Phoenix

When the Greek historian Herodotus (ca. 484–ca. 425 BCE) visited Egypt, he learned of the sacred *bennu* bird of Egyptian myth. He called it the phoenix, and wrote that it came to the Egyptian Temple of the Sun once every five hundred years. Later writers told a more complex story: every five centuries, the phoenix burned in a fire lit by the sun and then rose to begin life again. Inspired by this tale, many poets and artists have adopted the phoenix as a symbol of renewal and rebirth.

SCARAB (Right) In ancient Egypt, a mythic bird called the bennu was linked with creation, renewal, and the rising and setting sun. This quartzite scarab—an Egyptian amulet used to protect the living and the dead—depicts a bennu in a sacred boat on the right wing and the god of the underworld, Osiris, on the left. The scarab was embalmed with a mummy in ca. 1550–1186 BCE (New Kingdom).

Phœnix.

WHAT'S IN A NAME? (Left) Europeans once thought the Chinese mythical bird fenghuang was a close cousin of the legendary phoenix of the West. As it turns out, the two birds have separate mythic origins, although they continue to share the same English name. Here, an engraving of the Western phoenix from German encyclopedia writer Konrad Lykosthenes's *Prodigiorum ac Ostentorum Chronicon*, 1557.

WESTERN PHOENIX This painting from ca. 1720–50 by Dutch artist Cornelis Troost titled *The Phoenix* depicts the great bird rising from the ashes.

MYTHIC MORALS

Not all myths are just stories—many teach lessons. Characters in myths sometimes lead by example, reminding people how they should behave. Other times, mythic characters lie, cheat, or steal, and are then scolded or punished for their bad behavior. In Japan, people tell stories of *tengu*, part-bird, part-human goblinlike creatures of Buddhist and Shinto lore that live in the forests, mocking and punishing prideful people. The common Japanese expression *tengu ni naru* means "to become a tengu" and is used as a warning to not become arrogant.

Tengu are skilled swordsmen known to play tricks on arrogant Buddhist priests and to punish people who misuse knowledge or authority. According to some stories, people who are prideful or overconfident are reincarnated as tengu; only after a lifetime of good deeds can they be reborn as humans. Tengu were likely introduced to Japan from Korea and China between about 500 and 600 CE and were at first considered to be disruptive demons and omens of war. As late as 1860, the Japanese government posted official notices to tengu, asking the goblins to temporarily vacate a certain mountain during scheduled visits by the Shogun.

Over time, however, their image softened into one of mischievous mountain goblins. Today, tengu-like creatures are frequent characters in Japanese anime, a kind of cartoon.

MASK (Opposite top) Humanlike tengu can often be identified by their unnaturally long noses or red faces. This nineteenth-century Japanese mask is made of wood, lacquer, hair, and pigment.

MISCHIEVOUS MOUNTAIN GOBLINS

The earliest tengu had bird beaks, wings, and claws. Later tengu appear more humanlike but with long noses. In many stories, tengu wings are described as "shimmering." Tengu have supernatural abilities, including:

- Shape-shifting into human or animal forms
- Speaking without moving their mouths
- Moving instantly from place to place
- Appearing uninvited in people's dreams

Mountain Priests

Tengu are shape-shifters and can take many forms. But in legends, tengu are often described as having a human's body with wings and a long nose. And since the 1200s, humanlike tengu are often shown wearing the distinctive small, black cap and robe of a group of mountain-dwelling priests called *yamabushi*.

YAMABUSHI NETSUKE This nineteenth-century netsuke, a small toggle or fastener used to attach containers to clothing, is made of ivory, crystal, shell, wood, and pigment and carved in the shape of a tengu. Such birdlike tengu are often said to be born from giant eggs and live in high trees in the mountains.

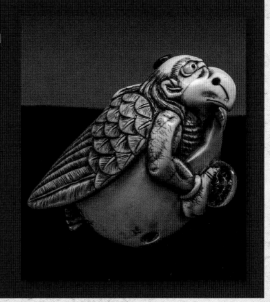

TENGU

Long ago, a man wandering through a forest in Japan came upon a long-nosed, magical goblin called a tengu. Eventually, the tengu agreed to teach the man *ninjitsu*, a kind of magic. Using ninjitsu, the man could now turn invisible, swim underwater for hours, or run as fast as a horse—just by uttering a few words. But the man was arrogant and soon began abusing his powers, using them to steal from travelers and sometimes even to kill them. One day as he was passing through the mountains, the man came upon a farmer walking slowly along the path. The man was impatient and would not wait for the farmer to move out of his way. He drew his sword and swung at the farmer's neck. But his sword never found its mark. Looking down, the man saw that his sword was broken. Looking up, he saw the farmer sitting in a tree laughing. The farmer was actually a tengu in disguise. Try as he might, the man could never perform ninjitsu again and was soon caught and punished.

—Adapted from a story told by Masaaki Miyazaki about his distant ancestor. Recorded by American folklorist Richard Dorson in 1957.

WOODBLOCK PRINT (Left) A long-nosed tengu is featured in this detail from a Japanese print from ca. 1830.

PILGRIM TENGU (Above) This colored print from ca. 1834, by Japanese master printmaker Hiroshige, is titled *Yellow Dusk*. It depicts a Shinto pilgrim entering the town of Numazu in eastern Shizuoka Prefecture, Japan, carrying a large tengu mask on his back.

DRAGONS

Creatures of Power

Of all the mythic creatures that rise from the water, prowl across land, or fly through the air, the dragon is the most famed. Stories of serpentlike beasts with fabulous powers inspire awe in almost every part of the world. Rain-bringing dragons in Asian tales can shrink so small that they fit in a teacup—or grow so large that they fill the sky. Dragons in Europe can slaughter people with their putrid breath, or spit fire and set cities ablaze. The earliest dragon legends date back thousands of years, and the creature still haunts our imagination today.

GRIM DESTROYER *Saint George and the Dragon,* from the workshop of Italian Renaissance painter Luca Signorelli, ca. 1495–1505.

Chapter 9

EUROPEAN & NEW WORLD DRAGONS

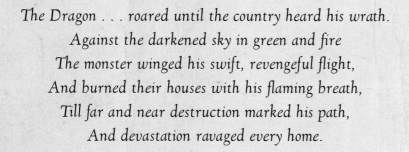

The Dragon . . . roared until the country heard his wrath.
Against the darkened sky in green and fire
The monster winged his swift, revengeful flight,
And burned their houses with his flaming breath,
Till far and near destruction marked his path,
And devastation ravaged every home.

—*Beowulf*, 700–1000 CE

WHERE DID THE DRAGON MYTH COME FROM? The dragons that lurk in European stories are powerful, wicked, and dangerous. In Christian tradition, they can symbolize Satan or sin. Some nest in caves and guard marvelous treasure. When hungry, they may snatch and devour sheep or cattle that wander too near. They may also eat humans—particularly young girls. Epic poems from the Middle Ages tell of warriors and knights who battle cruel and voracious dragons. In some stories, the hero slays his foe and wins fortune and honor. In others, he fails and is killed. The sinuous form of serpents and dragons has sparked the imagination of many artists over the ages and can still be seen today in various guises in popular culture, from books to movies to video games.

SATANIC DRAGONS
(Opposite) In the book of Revelation from the New Testament, dragons are often equated with Satan. Revelation 12:7 and 9 read in part: "And there was war in heaven: Michael and his angels fought against the dragon; and the dragon fought his angels. . . . And the great dragon was cast out, that old serpent, called the Devil, and Satan." Here, an Albrecht Dürer etching, *St. Michael Fighting the Dragon*, ca. 1498.

Here Be Dragons

European Dragon Facts

• In European tales, dragons often live deep inside caves, or in marshes near places where farm animals graze. Some sleep during the day and go on the rampage after night falls.

• May have wings.

• Kills people with its fiery, poisonous breath.

• Can strangle large animals with its tail.

• Creeps on four legs, two legs, or none.

European naturalists once considered the dragon a close relative of the snake, and both the snake and the dragon were once found in European books on natural history. In European stories, a dragonlike creature known as a *basilisk* was sometimes described as an enormous snake or lizard with a crown-shaped crest. Some authors called it the king of serpents and claimed it could kill a man with a single glance.

The legend of the Western dragon likely has roots in ancient Greece, where serpentlike monsters, often winged and sometimes many-headed, were featured in numerous myths (the word *dragon* comes from the Greek *drakōn*, meaning "serpent").

SOWING SOLDIERS (Right) In Greek mythology, the Greek hero Cadmus, the first king of Thebes, slayed a dragon, and at Athena's command sowed the dragon's teeth into the ground. A race of warriors sprung from the teeth, all but five of whom killed each other; the survivors helped Cadmus found Thebes. This engraving of the myth is from the Dutch workshop of Hendrik Goltzius, 1615.

LERNEAN HYDRA (Opposite) This Caeretan *hydria* (colorful ancient Greek vase), ca. 525 BCE, from Etruria (central Italy), depicts Heracles battling the Lernean Hydra, a many-headed serpent-dragon water monster of Greek mythology.

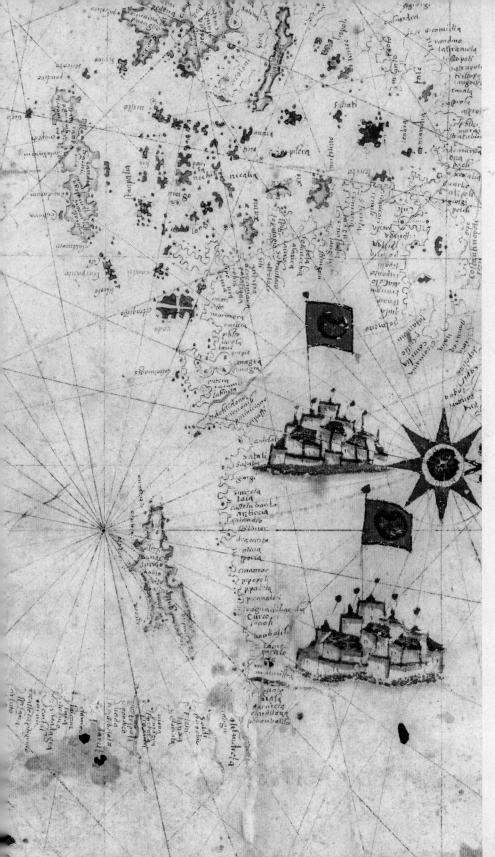

DRAGONS ON MAPS

Dragons were sometimes included on early maps to indicate dangerous, unknown, or unexplored areas, although the actual phrase "Here Be Dragons" is known to appear in Latin on only two sixteenth-century globes. Here, a dragon breathes fire on the outer corner of a portolan (navigational sea) chart of the Mediterranean and Black Seas by Italian cartographer Placido Oliva, ca. 1580.

Hic est Draco *ille alatus et quadripes omni ævo memorabilis, quem Deodatus de Gozon Eques Hierosolymitanus, in insula Rhodo eo quo descripsimus stratagemate confecit, qui et ob beneficium in Insulam collatum postmodum Magnus Ord. Magister creatus est.*

DRAGON COUNTRY In 1678, German naturalist Athanasius Kircher described the habits of dragons in his sweeping work on geology, *Mundus Subterraneus*, or *Subterranean World*. The book includes numerous illustrations of dragons, such as the one of the four-legged specimen above. Another illustration (opposite top) shows the legendary dragons of Mount Pilatus, Switzerland, which were said to cause terrible storms. The opposite bottom image portrays a local hero: around 1250 CE, the Swiss knight Heinrich von Winkelried reportedly killed a belligerent dragon, but died after touching its poisonous blood.

Lacus
Pilati

Mons Pilati

Lacus
Lucernen
sis
pars

Dracken feldt

Antru
Draconis

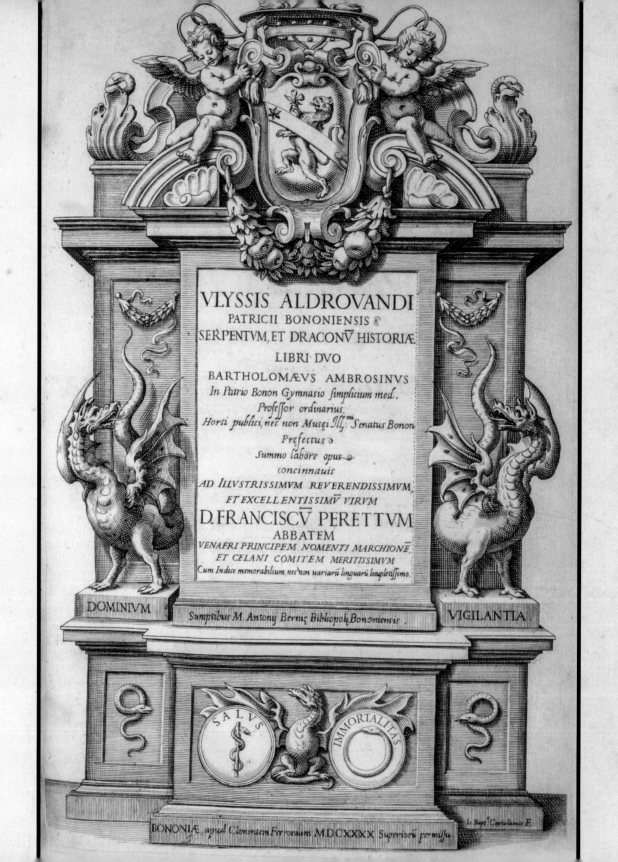

VLYSSIS ALDROVANDI
PATRICII BONONIENSIS &
SERPENTVM, ET DRACONV HISTORIÆ
LIBRI DVO
BARTHOLOMÆVS AMBROSINVS
In Patrio Bonon Gymnasio simplicium med.
Professor ordinarius,
Horti publici, nec non Musei Ill.mi Senatus Bonon.
Prefectus
Summo labore opus
concinnauit
AD ILLVSTRISSIMVM REVERENDISSIMVM,
ET EXCELLENTISSIMV VIRVM
D. FRANCISCV PERETTVM
ABBATEM
VENAFRI PRINCIPEM NOMENTI MARCHIONE,
ET CELANI COMITEM MERITISSIMVM
Cum Indice memorabilium, nec non uariarū linguarū locuplerissimo.

Sumptibus M. Antonij Bernij Bibliopolæ Bononiensis

DOMINIVM

VIGILANTIA

SALVS

IMMORTALITAS

BONONIÆ, apud Clementem Ferronium MDCXXXX Superiorū permissu.

Io. Bapt. Coriolanus F.

SERPENT KING European naturalists once considered the dragon a close relative of the snake. In his work *Serpentum et Draconum Historiae* (1640), Ulisse Aldrovandi, a professor of natural science at the University of Bologna, discussed the dragon's habits and environments. Right, a detail of an engraving of a crowned basilisk, the "king of serpents," from *Serpentum*, and below, a winged dragon. Opposite, the frontispiece from the book.

"Winged dragons flying through Africa beat enormous animals such as bulls to death with their tails."

—Ulisse Aldrovandi,
Serpentum et Draconum Historiae, 1640

Draco alatus Apes ex Greuino.

SAINT GEORGE AND THE DRAGON

The legendary dragon slayer Saint George is a popular symbol of the Christian faith. Saint George was believed to have lived sometime in the third century. Likely born in ancient Cappadocia, in an area of what is now Turkey, he was said to be a Roman soldier who was beheaded for refusing to renounce his faith. The story of Saint George and the dragon was first written down in ca. 1260 in the *Golden Legend*, a book of saints' lives by Jacobus de Varagine, the archbishop of Genoa, and became more widespread when translations of that book were printed after the 1450s. In the story, George rescues a Libyan princess from being sacrificed to a dragon that has been terrorizing her city. He agrees to kill the dragon if the princess, her father, and their subjects agree to be baptized.

RELIGIOUS TEXT (Left) Saint George has long been venerated in the Ethiopian Orthodox Church, which has roots reaching back more than 1,700 years. His image decorates this frontispiece of a New Testament book, the Letters of Saint Paul, date unknown.

MILITARY SAINT (Opposite) In this painting by noted Flemish artist Rogier van der Weyden, ca. 1432–35, the princess looks on as Saint George, in full battle armor, pierces the dragon with his lance.

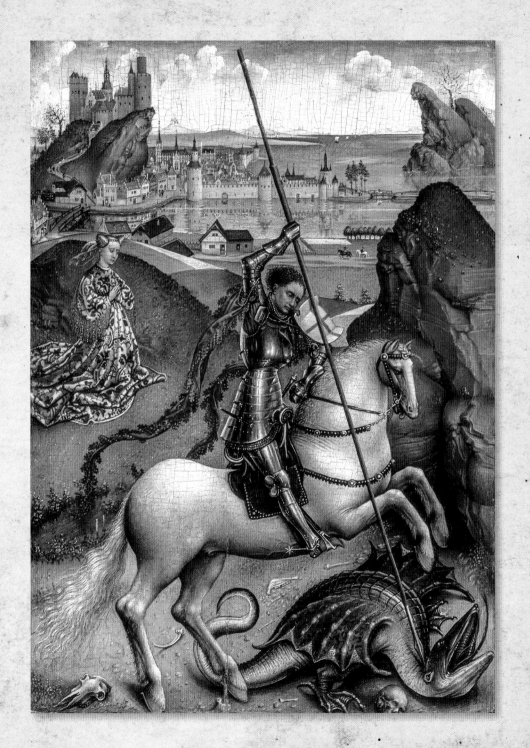

"S. George was a knight and born in Cappadocia. On a time he came to the province of Libya, to a city which is said Silene. And by this city was a stagne or a pond like the sea, wherein was a dragon which envenomed all the country."

—*Golden Legend*, Jacobus de Varagine, William Caxton, translator (1483), edition from 1900

DOMINE DIRIGE NOS

London.

Unser Kaifer an fein Volk

„Eine schwere Stunde ist heute über Deutschland hereingebrochen. Neider überall zwingen uns zu gerechter Verteidigung. Man drückt uns das Schwert in die Hand. Ich hoffe, daß wir, wenn es nicht in letzter Stunde meinen Bemühungen gelingt, die Gegner zum Einsehen zu bringen und den Frieden zu erhalten, das Schwert mit Gottes Hilfe so führen werden, daß wir es mit Ehren wieder in die Scheide stecken können. Enorme Opfer an Gut und Blut würde ein Krieg vom deutschen Volke fordern, den Gegnern aber würden wir zeigen, was es heißt, Deutschland anzugreifen. Und nun empfehle ich Euch Gott. Jetzt geht in die Kirche, kniet nieder vor Gott und bittet ihn um Hilfe für unser braves Heer!" Berlin, 31. Juli 1914.

BRITAIN · NEEDS
YOU · AT · ONCE

PUBLISHED BY THE PARLIAMENTARY RECRUITING COMMITTEE, LONDON. POSTER No 108.   PRINTED BY SPOTTISWOODE & Cº Lᵀᴰ LONDON. E.C.

COIN (Opposite top) Dragon-killing saints adorn coins from Christian kingdoms but can also be found in the Islamic world. In Turkey and Syria, the Christian Saint George is sometimes revered as al-Khidr, a Muslim patron of spring and fertility. Saint George, the patron saint of England, adorns this gold coin from Tudor England, ca. 1544–47.

HERALDRY (Opposite bottom) During the Middle Ages, dragons became popular figures in heraldry, appearing on banners, seals, and other emblems of authority and military might. Here, a nineteenth-century engraving of the coat of arms of London.

A FAMILIAR FACE The dragon has remained a potent symbol of treachery well into the industrial age. Dragons were often used on political posters and in political cartoons. During World War I, both the British and the Germans created posters depicting the enemy as a dragon to be slayed by Saint George. The German poster, above left, is from 1914, and Saint George represents Kaiser Wilhelm II. The text below the drawing reads "Our Emperor to his people." The British poster, above right, 1915, is an appeal to enlist.

New World Dragon: Quetzalcoatl

XOCHICALCO (Below) The winding form of Quetzalcoatl was carved in the wall of a temple at Xochicalco, Mexico, the capital of a wealthy kingdom between 600 and 900 CE. Many early pictures of the feathered serpent resemble the dragons of Asia and Europe. One reason that snakelike creatures appear in so many myths of the world might be that the snake's long, sinuous body and rippling movement suggest flowing water, a source of life.

In the ancient Mesoamerican city of Xochicalco, in Mexico, a temple stands in ruins. Stone snakeheads with gaping jaws guard the steps to the top. The god who was worshiped here, at the Temple of the Feathered Serpent, was called Quetzalcoatl, or "feathered serpent." This god appeared in many forms. He often had the sharp fangs, fiery gaze, and winding body of a snake—and the deep green feathers of the quetzal, a tropical bird. In Aztec religion, Quetzalcoatl was linked with the sky: with the rain, the wind, and the movement of the planet Venus. Like the dragons of Europe and Asia, he was also a symbol of power for priests and kings.

SERPENT HEAD (Above) Serpent heads similar to the one shown here stare out from a temple at Teotihuacán, Mexico, a lavish city that rose and fell between 1 and 700 CE. These stone sculptures are some of the oldest images known of the dragonlike deity honored by the ancient civilizations of Mexico and Central America. No one knows what he was called by the residents of Teotihuacán, but his Aztec name was Quetzalcoatl, and the Mayans knew him as K'uk'ulkan. Both names can be translated as "feathered snake" or "plumed serpent."

Quetzalcoatl
Dios particular
delos de Chulu-
la.

TOVAR CODEX This illustration of Quetzalcoatl is from the *Tovar Codex*, an illustrated manuscript about the history and culture of the Aztec people created by Mexican Jesuit Juan de Tovar in ca. 1585. De Tovar was the son of a captain who traveled to the New World with Spanish conquistador Pánfilo de Narváez.

TEMPLE OF QUETZALCOATL (Following pages) A detail of the Temple of Quetzalcoatl at Teotihuacán.

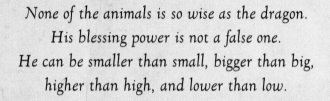

Chapter 10
ASIAN DRAGONS

None of the animals is so wise as the dragon.
His blessing power is not a false one.
He can be smaller than small, bigger than big,
higher than high, and lower than low.

—Chinese scholar Lu Dian (1042–1102)

THE DRAGONS OF EAST ASIAN LEGEND HAVE SWEEPING POWERS.
They breathe clouds, move the seasons, and control the waters of rivers, lakes, and
seas. They are linked with yang, the masculine principle of heat, light, and action,
and opposed to yin, the feminine principle of coolness, darkness, and repose.
Dragons have been part of East Asian culture for more than four thousand years.
In the religious traditions of Buddhism, Confucianism, and Taoism, they have been
honored as sources of power and bringers of rain.

JAPANESE DRAGONS
(Opposite) Detail of a
woodcut of two dragons
by Japanese printmaker
Utagawa Yoshitsuya,
ca. 1843.

Imperial Dragon

Imperial Dragon Facts

• Bump on the forehead called a *chi mu* helps the dragon float up to the heavens.

• Eighty-one scales, equal to nine multiplied by nine—nine is a lucky number in China.

• Sweet-smelling saliva.

• Excellent eyesight.

• Four legs with up to five claws on each foot, but typically no wings.

• Chinese dragons live underwater in winter. In spring, they rise to the sky and make rain.

Small as a silkworm or broad as the sky, magnificent dragons are said to dwell in the rivers, lakes, and seas of China. Every spring, they rise from the waters and curl and twist through the sky, breathing clouds and sending rain to make farmers' fields green. In Chinese tradition, the master of the waters is sometimes known as the "dragon king." Lobsters and shrimp are his courtiers, and he lives in a palace at the bottom of the sea.

Revered above all other creatures in East Asian tradition, the dragon is also a symbol of imperial rule. The Chinese emperor was known as the "dragon." His hands were the dragon's claws, and his seat was the dragon throne. United with heaven and earth, a wise emperor ruled in harmony with the cosmos and brought peace and prosperity to all.

SHADOW PUPPETS (Right) The dragon king and his court play a magical role in shadow puppet shows, once popular on the streets of Beijing. In a shadow puppet play, performers stand behind a screen of cloth or paper and use bamboo rods to move puppets, props, and scenery. A lamp shining from behind the painted puppets casts a colored shadow on the screen, which is all the audience sees. In one classic shadow play, the legendary woman warrior Liu Jinding falls in love with a handsome general and demands that he marry her. When he resists, the dragon king comes to her aid, causing a flood that threatens to drown the reluctant bridegroom. This nineteenth-century puppet from Beijing is made of donkey hide, iron, cotton, dye, and tung oil.

DRAGON KING (Above) An ink-stick print of the Chinese dragon king rising into the clouds from his palace at the bottom of the sea, from a book titled *Cheng shi mo y van* (*The Ink Garden of the Cheng Family*) (1594–1606) by an ink-stick maker named Cheng Chun-Fang.

PRECIOUS PEARL

Imperial robes and other East Asian works of art often show the dragon with a pearl surrounded by branching flames (center of image). Some scholars view the pearl as a symbol of rolling thunder, belched from the dragon's mouth as it reaches the sky. Others regard it as a luminous "pearl of potentiality," a philosophical sign linked with Taoist ideas of the ever changing and indefinite. This gilded, jade book cover is for *The Song of the Jade Bowl*, 1745, by the Qianlong Emperor (1711–99).

"*The dragon's horns resemble those of a stag, his head that of a camel, his eyes those of a demon, his neck that of a snake, his belly that of a clam, his scales those of a carp, his claws those of an eagle, his soles those of a tiger, his ears those of a cow.*"

—Han dynasty Chinese scholar
Wang Fu, ca. 82–167 CE

FORBIDDEN PALACE This dragon is part of the tile wall called the Nine-Dragon Screen, erected in 1773 at the Palace of Tranquil Longevity in the Forbidden City—the site of the imperial palace in Beijing and the seat of imperial government in China (1420–1912).

Dragon Robes

Chinese dragons are said to spend winter on the floor of a lake or the ocean. Each spring they rise to the heavens, creating a clap of thunder, to form clouds and water the land. The dragons embroidered on imperial robes are often shown soaring up to the sky from the sea, represented by the broad expanse of diagonal lines near the hem.

The Chinese dragon is a powerful force, and its influence has spread well beyond China's borders. When the empire was flourishing, Chinese rulers often sent richly embroidered dragon robes to neighboring kingdoms as a gesture of good will and diplomacy (see page 168). These garments radiated so much power, they were sometimes venerated—and often imitated.

WOMAN'S ROBE (Right) For more than a thousand years, Chinese emperors wore robes decorated with bold dragon designs. Under Qing dynasty (1644–1911/12) laws, only the emperor and his immediate family were allowed to wear the five-clawed dragon, or *long*, embroidered on the nineteenth-century silk robe shown here. Those of lower rank had to settle for dragons with fewer claws—though by the end of the dynasty, these rules were often ignored. Some dragon robes were made for the theater, with features exaggerated for colorful effect on the stage.

BRIDEGROOM'S COAT (Right) Chinese dragon designs appear in the spectacular textile arts of the Nanai people, who live along the far-eastern Chinese-Russian border. Pieced from many fragments of silk and cotton cloth, this nineteenth-century wedding coat captures the spirit of the dragon robes worn by emperors of the Qing dynasty. Patches of color form scales on the back, bits of brocade cut from a dragon robe mark the shoulders, and wavy stripes suggest water at the hem.

DRAGON RULE (Left) This eighteenth-century engraving by Flemish printmaker Lambertus Antonius Claessens depicts the Qianlong Emperor of China, who reigned from 1735 to 1796. The image is from the book *An Authentic Account of an Embassy from the King of Great Britain to the Emperor of China*, ca. 1798–1801, a travelogue documenting the Macartney Embassy, the first British diplomatic mission to China in 1793, led by George Macartney, 1st Earl Macartney. The Qianlong Emperor wears a dragon-embellished robe, a symbol of his omnipotent rule.

DRAGON SON

LONG AGO, THERE WAS a poor farmer who lived in a wild and rugged land, far from the great cities of China. One day when he was coming home from the fields, he came to a pond. There he stopped and stared in amazement. On the banks of the pond lay his wife, fast asleep. A great scaly dragon loomed above her. Clouds blackened the sky, lightning flashed, and the air shook with thunder. Months later, when the farmer's wife gave birth to a beautiful son, the couple were filled with joy. This boy grew up to become Emperor Gaozu, the first ruler of the Han dynasty (206 BCE–220 CE).

—Adapted from a story recounted by Chinese scholar Sima Qian in *Shiji* (*Historical Records*), ca. 109–91 BCE

GREAT SCALY DRAGON
An illustration from a sixteenth-century Chinese book titled *The Ink Garden of the Cheng Family* (see page 150).

HAPPY COUPLE (Below) In Chinese art, the dragon is sometimes paired with another legendary creature, the *fenghuang*—or phoenix (see page 118)—shown here in an illustration from *The Ink Garden of the Cheng Family*. Both are considered auspicious symbols. Together, the phoenix and dragon are often equated with the harmony of marriage and the union of complementary cosmic elements yin and yang. During the Ming dynasty (1368–1644), the phoenix became a symbol for the empress—the bride of the dragon.

DRAGON RAMP (Above) This stone ramp in the center of the stairway to the Hall of Supreme Harmony—built during the Ming dynasty at the Forbidden Palace in Beijing—is engraved with dragons, symbols of the emperor. The emperor's litter would be carried over the ramp during ceremonial processions.

"*There once was a king with magical powers who ruled the kingdom of Kuqa, near the western border of China. In those days, the markets were rich in gold, silver, and precious gems. But one night, a mischievous dragon turned these treasures to charcoal, and the wealth of the kingdom was lost. So the king struck back. He took up his sword, tracked down the dragon, and leaped on its back. Furious, the dragon belched fire like lightning, then soared to the sky. The king remained calm. 'If you don't surrender,' he quietly told the dragon, 'I'll cut off your head.' 'Please don't kill me!' the dragon cried. 'I'll take you wherever you want to go!' And from that time on, the king traveled by dragon instead of by horse, flying swiftly all over the realm.*"

—Based on a story told along the Silk Road, recorded by Chinese scholar Li Fang (925–96 CE)

QUICK CHANGE (Right) In East Asian stories, the dragon is a master of transformation. It can shrink, stretch, or disappear—or take the form of a fish, snake, or human being. In this early-twentieth-century illustration of a legend about Chinese Zen Buddhist sage Huineng (638–713 CE), Huineng persuades a fierce and destructive dragon to shrink small enough to fit into his rice bowl.

MOVING IMAGE (Opposite) Chinese images and ideas have spread to other lands through friendly ties—and sometimes through war and conquest. Although the dragon in this scene (a miniature from a 1604 edition of the epic poem *Shahnameh* [*Book of Kings*]) illustrates a Persian tale, it has a Chinese look. The dragon is one of many artistic forms that passed from China to Persia (present-day Iran) in the 1200s, when both countries were conquered and controlled by the Mongols.

CHINESE DRAGON DANCE

The dragon dance is a Chinese tradition linked with the Lunar New Year. In Chinese communities all over the world, performers celebrate the season by parading through the streets holding poles that sinuously move a long, brightly colored dragon made of bamboo, cloth, and paper. This custom may have ancient roots. The dragon is a symbol of spring, and its image has been used in rain ceremonies dating back at least to the Han dynasty.

EIGHT-MAN DRAGON DANCE A Japanese print, ca. 1880, depicting a Chinese dragon dance.

"*The dragon's nature is rough and fierce, and yet he likes beautiful gems and the Stone of Darkness, and is fond of roasted swallow flesh. He is afraid of iron, the wang plant, of centipedes, of the leaves of the lien tree, and of five-colored silk thread.*"

—Chinese scholar Li Shizhen
(1518–93)

NEW YORK DRAGON (Above) The parade dragon seen here was made in Hong Kong and has made many public appearances, carried by dancers from the Wan Chi Ming Hung Gar Institute, a martial arts school in New York City.

CHINATOWN PARADE (Below) Detail of Chinese dragon in a parade in San Francisco, ca. 2014.

MAP OF ASIAN DRAGONS

CHINA One of China's most subtle delicacies is Longjing (Dragon Well) tea, named for a tea-growing region near Hangzhou, in Zhejiang Province. It is said that centuries ago, people believed that a rain-bringing dragon lived in the area at the bottom of a clear, running spring.

BORNEO In a folktale from Malaysian Borneo, a dragon is said to guard a precious jewel on the top of Mount Kinabalu.

VIETNAM According to Vietnamese legend, the rocky islands of Ha Long Bay were spat out by a dragon that guarded the country in ancient times. The name of the bay means "descending dragon."

JAPAN A dragon king was once said to live in a pond at Shinsen-en, the imperial garden of Kyoto, Japan. During times of drought, Buddhist monks held ceremonies there to persuade the dragon king to rise and bring rain.

KOREA A long, low mountain called Naksan in the shape of a blue dragon lies to the east of the old city center of Seoul, South Korea. A higher one, Inwangsan, once called White Tiger Mountain, stands to the west. The Korean capital was founded some six hundred years ago below these peaks, an auspicious spot according to the principles of spatial planning known in Korean as *p'ungsu* (feng shui).

DOOR PROTECTOR (Left) Chinese door handle decorated with a five-clawed dragon, ca. 1600, used to ward off evil spirits.

CLOUD DRAGON (Below) This Japanese woodcut of a dragon materializing out of a cloud is from ca. 1900.

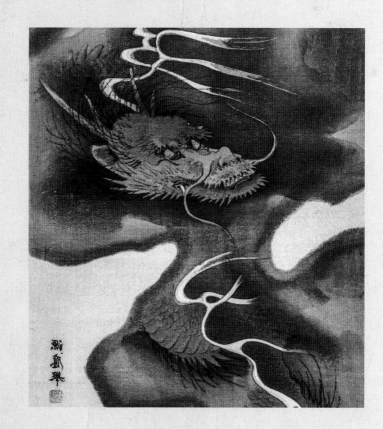

DRAGONS OF JAPAN

Japanese dragon mythology is rooted in that of China, and was likely transmitted to the island country via the spread of Buddhism, which reached Japan around the sixth century CE. Japanese dragons resemble Chinese ones: typically wingless and serpentine, with clawed feet. While dragon myths in Japan are centuries old, they continue to make magic in popular culture. In the popular Japanese anime series *Dragon Ball Z*, for example, the dragon Shenron has the power to grant wishes.

SWORD GUARD (Above) Samurai warriors used *tsuba*, or sword guards, to protect their hands during combat. Later sword guards were finely decorated, often with classic Chinese or Japanese symbols or scenes. On the copper alloy and gold Edo-period (1603–1867) *tsuba* shown here, a dragon carries Lu Dongbin, one of the legendary figures in Taoist tradition known as the Eight Immortals.

BODY ARMOR (Right) Worn into battle by Samurai warriors, the dragon was used in Japan as an emblem of strength and power. Japanese families still celebrate the same spirit during Children's Day (once called Boys' Day) each May 5th, decorating their homes with, among other items, a miniature display of warrior figures and other symbols of combat, including a sword, helmet, and suit of armor. This iron breastplate is from the Edo period.

SAMURAI (Opposite) Three samurai pose in armor in this image by noted Japanese photographer Kusakabe Kimbei, ca. 1875.

福通屋内成

　釣日さ次庭の
障子のよ
り雲つ
敷の部くる
知ら枝の　梅
　　　　六樹園

うつ枝の
うつうたか〱〱
　　龍〵仏を
ほよけにる〱る
あらきら
　　　の春

KOTO PLAYER (Opposite)
A print by Gogaku Yajima, ca. 1820, depicting a woman playing a *koto* (stringed musical instrument) with a dragon curling around her legs.

WARRIOR PRINT (Left)
Warrior Tado no Manchu on horseback shooting an arrow into a dragon flying out of a river, in a print by *ukiyo-e* (woodblock) master Taiso Yoshitoshi, ca. 1880.

THE DRAGON IN MANY LANDS

For many centuries, Chinese emperors sent robes and bolts of satin covered with dragon designs to rulers in Korea, Vietnam, Thailand, Burma (present-day Myanmar), Mongolia, and many other neighboring countries. In some areas, people made ceremonial clothing that echoed the imperial robes, adapting the dragon to local traditions. With these gifts intended to maintain ties, the Chinese image of the dragon spread across much of East and Central Asia.

"Last year you bestowed on me a mang [four-clawed dragon] robe. I placed it on the sleeping couch, and morning and evening I raised my hands and worshipped it. But I was afraid, and did not dare to wear it. Now I am preparing to venerate the former kings, and I am about to wear it in order to honor my ancestors."

—From a letter sent by King Seonjo of Korea
to Emperor Wanli of China, 1588

DRAGON DRUM This Buddhist temple in South Korea is painted in the traditional Korean style of *Dancheong*: elaborately decorated patterns painted on architecture using bright primary colors. Buddhist ceremonial drums—such as this one painted with a Korean dragon—are often suspended in temple entrances.

DRAGON AND CARP In a popular Chinese legend that spread to other parts of Asia, thousands of koi fish (carp) try to leap up a waterfall, known as the Dragon's Gate, on the Yellow River. With brave determination, one fish succeeds—and is instantly transformed into a dragon. This Korean painting from the early twentieth century shows a magnificent dragon along with three peacefully swimming carp. The carp with the red mouth is the one destined to be transformed.

TEMPLE DRAGON
(Opposite) Snakelike dragons decorate the roofs and rafters of many Korean temples, such as this one, helping carry prayers up to heaven.

DRAGON STATUE (Below) A large dragon statue stands guard outside of Haedong Yonggungsa, a Buddhist temple in Busan, South Korea, dating back to 1376.

HOUSE RAFTER (Above) On the island of Borneo in Southeast Asia, the traditional houses of the Kayan and Kenyah people have long verandas with crouching dragon shapes carved in the rafters above. The artist who created the flowing dragon design here, from the early 1900s, may have borrowed ideas from porcelain jars brought to the island by Chinese traders. In Borneo, the dragon is a goddess of the underworld. She protects the living, guards over the dead, and is associated with earth, water, thunder, and lightning.

THAI DEITY (Left) In Asian legends, emperors, philosophers, gods, and saints often travel by dragon. In this Thai painting from a ca. 1870 manuscript, a Hindu deity rides a blue dragon.

DRAGON AND GODDESS (Opposite) This nineteenth-century copper alloy and gilt statuette depicts a dragon carrying the mountain spirit Dorje Lumo, adopted by Tibetan Buddhists as one of the twelve Tenma, guardian goddesses of the Buddhist tradition.

肝神名龍煙字含明

肝之狀為龍主藏

魂象如懸匏色如

縞映絓生心下而

近後右四葉左三

葉脈出于大敦大

敦左大指端三毛

之中也

圖

Chapter 11
DRAGONS & NATURAL HISTORY

The dragons of the mountains have scales of a golden color, and in length excel those of the plain, and they have bushy beards, which also are of a golden hue; and their eye is sunk deep under the eyebrow, and emits a terrible and ruthless glance.

—Greek scholar Philostratus (ca. 170–245 CE),
Life of Apollonius of Tyana

IN LEGENDS AND FOLKTALES, DRAGONS ARE MAGICAL—yet early naturalists often treated these creatures as part of the physical world. Chinese scholars had classified the dragon as one of the 369 animal species with scales. Biologists and naturalists in Europe once wrote accounts of the behavior and habitat of dragons, along with lizards and snakes (see page 132). Long before the development of paleontology, people unearthed fossilized bones in Asia and Europe—and believed they had found the remains of dragons from an earlier age.

DRAGON LIVER (Opposite) This woodcut is from a Chinese Ming dynasty encyclopedia published in 1609, titled *Sancai Tuhui* (*Illustrations of the Three Powers*), by the authors Wang Qi and his son Wang Siyi. The spirit of the liver is depicted in the form of a dragon; so-called dragon's teeth (pulverized dinosaur fossils) were said to be a remedy for liver ailments.

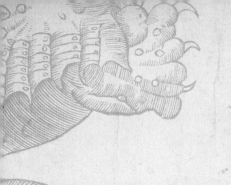

Dragons in the Dust

DRAGON BONES

In traditional Chinese medicine, *longgu,* or "dragon bones," are prescribed as a treatment for numerous ailments, from madness to diarrhea and dysentery. Most fragments and powders sold in Chinese pharmacies as dragon bone come from fossil remains of extinct mammals, unearthed from China's renowned fossil beds.

"For using dragon's bones, first cook odorous plants; bathe the bones twice in hot water, pound them to powder and put this in bags of gauze. Take a couple of young swallows and, after taking out their intestines and stomach, put the bags in the swallows and hang them over a well. After one night take the bags out of the swallows, rub the powder, and mix it into medicines for strengthening the kidneys. The efficacy of such a medicine is as it were divine!"

—Chinese medical scholar
Lei Xiao (420–477 CE)

BONES OF ROCK (Left) These "dragon bone" samples from China, ca. 1900, bought by a collector unfamiliar with Chinese medicine, are actually just ordinary rocks.

BONES IN THE FIELD (Opposite) Naturalist and explorer Roy Chapman Andrews (former director of the American Museum of Natural History, 1934–42) and vertebrate paleontologist Walter W. Granger with dinosaur bones, Third Asiatic Expedition, Mongolia, ca. 1928.

 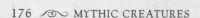

DRAGONS AND *T. REX* With their enormous size, reptilian shape, and threatening teeth and claws, some dragons might easily be taken for cousins of *Tyrannosaurus rex* (shown here, the bones of a *Tyrannosaurus rex* discovered in Big Dry Creek, Montana, by Museum paleontologist Barnum Brown in 1902 and 1908, exhibited in the Hall of Saurischian Dinosaurs at the American Museum of Natural History). Living dinosaurs did not inspire the dragon idea—they died out long before people were around to observe them. But the fossil remains of extinct animals have sometimes been mistaken for dragon bones—and helped perpetuate old dragon stories.

PREPARING FOR DISPLAY Charles Lang, Jeremiah Walsh, Charles Hoffman, and Paul Bultman working on *Tyrannosaurus rex* skulls at the American Museum of Natural History, in the 1920s.

TOWN TROPHY (Left) Legend has it that long ago, the marshes near Klagenfurt, Austria, were haunted by a fearsome *lindwurm*—a serpentlike Germanic dragon. (In Germanic and Norse mythology, lindwurms could be with or without legs, and with or without wings.) It devoured all the people and livestock who ventured its way. Finally, a local ruler called on his knights to destroy the dragon, and after many attempts it was slain. To commemorate the event, a "dragon" skull was placed in the town hall. In 1582, an artist borrowed the skull—really the fossil remains of an Ice Age woolly rhinoceros—to use as a model in shaping a massive six-ton fountain sculpture of the lindwurm, which still stands in the city today.

"DRAGON" SKULL (Below) The skull of a woolly rhinoceros (*Coelodonta antiquitatis*), such as the one shown here (cast), was once kept in the town hall of Klagenfurt, Austria. It was said to be the remains of a dragon slain before the city was founded ca. 1250. (Note: the skull is missing its distinctive horns.)

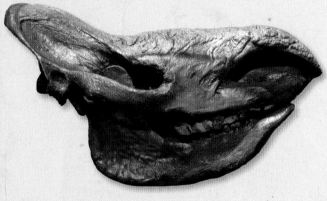

Dragon's Blood

In ancient times, Arab merchants once sailed to the Socotra Islands (part of present-day Yemen) in the Arabian Sea to obtain this resin from the fruit of the palmlike "dragon's blood tree," *Dracaena cinnabari*. In the fifteenth century, Europeans also began obtaining the resin from *Dracaena draco* in the Canary Islands. Dragon's blood was once prized as a medicine in Europe and the Middle East. According to the Roman naturalist Pliny the Elder (23–79 CE), it formed when dragons attacked elephants, and their blood ran together and congealed.

RESIN (Above) Balls of "dragon's blood" resin from the *Dracaena cinnabari* plant, native to the Socotra Islands, Yemen.

DRAGON'S BLOOD TREE (Right) Photograph of a *Dracaena cinnabari* in Socotra, from *The Natural History of Sokotra and Abd-el-Kuri*, 1903. The photograph was taken by Scottish explorer and Liverpool Museum director Henry Ogg Forbes, editor of the book.

"*The word kinnabari, [Pliny] says, is properly the name given to the thick matter which issues from the dragon when crushed beneath the weight of the dying elephant. . . . The occasions were the continual combat which were believed to take place between the two. The dragon was said to have a passion for elephant's blood; he twined himself around the elephant's trunk, fixed his teeth behind the ear, and drained all the blood at a draught.*"

—The Periplus of the Erythraean Sea: Travel and Trade in the Indian Ocean by a Merchant of the First Century, Wilfred H. Schoff, translator, 1912 edition

MORTAL ENEMIES

A dragon and an elephant fight to the death in this illustration from medieval England, ca. 1250. According to the Roman scholar Pliny the Elder, a dragon could strangle an elephant with its tail. Perhaps Pliny heard stories about pythons, which can crush and devour large animals, though elephants are beyond their capabilities.

Acanthus   Callionymus

TEEMING SEA This print by Nicolaes de Bruyn, ca. 1600, is populated with numerous "sea monsters"—gigantic fish—and in the foreground, a hippocampus.

Acknowledgments

Mythic Creatures: And the Impossibly Real Animals Who Inspired Them would not have been possible without the support of the staff and trustees of the American Museum of Natural History.

This book was based on the exhibition *Mythic Creatures: Dragons, Unicorns & Mermaids*, created by the American Museum of Natural History under the direction of David Harvey, Senior Vice President for Exhibition. This book is largely drawn from the exhibition text, written by Margaret Dornfeld, Martin Schwabacher, and John Whitney, with Sasha Nemecek, Senior Editor, and Lauri Halderman, Senior Director of Exhibition Interpretation.

This book could not have been created without the knowledge and assistance of the Museum's scientific and curatorial staff, including Laurel Kendall, Mark A. Norell, and Richard Ellis.

From Sterling Publishing, Executive Editor Barbara Berger brought this book to fruition, with assistance from Senior Art Director Chris Thompson, Senior Art Director Elizabeth Lindy, Creative Director Jo Obarowski, Production Director Fred Pagan, and Editorial Director Marilyn Kretzer; cover designer Patrice Kaplan; and Ashley Prine and Katherine Furman at Tandem Books.

Much hard work and support was provided by the Museum's Exhibition and Global Business Development departments, with many thanks to Elizabeth Hormann, Kate Reutershan, Joanna Livingstone, and Sharon Stulberg, Senior Director. Additional support was offered by the Museum's Research Library staff, particularly Senior Research Services Librarian Mai Reitmeyer and Harold Boeschenstein Director Tom Baione.

Many thanks to the Museum's Division of Anthropology and Barry Landua, Systems Manager/Manager of Digital Imaging.

The talented and hardworking staff of the Museum's photography studio were generous with their assistance, especially Denis Finnin, Director.

And last, but certainly not least, a great deal of gratitude is extended to Jill Hamilton for her careful proofreading and many helpful queries, comments, and suggestions along the way.

Index

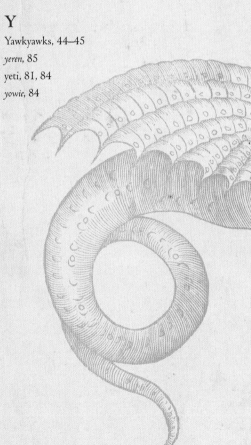

Picture Credits

t: top; b: bottom; c: center; r: right; l: left

COVER (design by Patrice Kaplan and Elizabeth Lindy)
FRONT: Left (St. George and the Dragon) and center (griffin):
Digital images courtesy of the Getty's Open Content Program
BACKGROUND front, spine, and back: © Labetskiy Alexandr/
Shutterstock (vine pattern); © wanchai/Shutterstock (parchment)
TOP front, spine, and back (tentacles): American Museum of
Natural History Research Library, Call #RF-29-F
SPINE bottom: Wellcome Library, London
BACK bottom center: American Museum of Natural History
Division of Anthropology, Catalog #70.0/7502

Front endpapers: Courtesy Library of Congress Prints and
Photographs Division, LC-USZC4-10363
Back endpapers: American Museum of Natural History Research
Library, Call #C-3

AGE Fotostock
©ARCO/R. Hicker/AGE Fotostock

Alamy
© Mary Evans Picture Library/Alamy Stock Photo: 11; © MCLA
Collection/Alamy: 29tr; © Black Star/Alamy Stock Photo: 39;
© Dale O'Dell/Alamy Stock Photo: 80

© American Museum of Natural History
DIVISION OF ANTHROPOLOGY: Catalog #70/10076: ix(b);
Catalog #41.2/5800: 23; Catalog #41.2/7979: 26bl;
Catalog #70.3/6507: 29tl; Catalog #A/741 A-CL: 76bl;
Catalog #70.3/542, Drummond collection: 78tr;
Catalog #70.0/902: 79tr; Catalog #70.0/3676: 79bl;
Catalog #70.0/7502: 107; Catalog #70.0/8095: 109l;
Catalog #70.0/8092: 115bl; Catalog #70/11388: 118;
Catalog #70.3/3760: 119b; Catalog #70.3/5364: 121r;
Catalog #70.0/3674: 125t; Catalog #70.3/545: 125b;
Catalog #90.2/5400: 140b; Catalog #30.0/6169: 144cr;
Catalog #70/10081: 150–51b; Catalog #70.2/5296: 154–55bc;
Catalog #70/580: 155tr; Catalog #70.2/1230 F: 164t,

Catalog #70.2/1230: 164b; Catalog #70.2/2102: 172t;
Catalog #70.0/7560: 173; Catalog #70/13848: 176b;
Image #129039: 179

EXHIBITION DEPARTMENT: 14 (whale and squid imagery), 34–35
(map), 84–85 (map), 162–63 (map)

DENIS FINNIN: 10c, 59b, 62, 65t, 86b, 87c, 105l, 161tr, 178, 181

RODERICK MICKENS: 58

PHOTO STUDIO: viii, xii, 12, 60tr, 102, 105tr

RESEARCH LIBRARY: Image #3394: v; Call #B-6: xi; Call #RF-
29-E: xiv; Call #J-4: 1; Call #RF-74-F: 5; Call #RF-29-F: 10 (far
left); Call #A-1a: 16tl; Call #RF-29-E: 16br; Call #B-6: 17; Call
#QL89.O9: 21t; Image #23373: 43 (center); Call #J-4: 54br;
Image #410737: 59t; Image #3158: 61t; Call #DD-4: 70; Call
#58-E: 76 (center right); Call #B-6: 122 (left); Call #RF-43-G:
136t; Call #RF-43-G: 137; Call #RF-1-J: 138; Call #RF-1-J:
139t; Call #RF-1-J: 139b; Laufer Collection #565: 150tr, 156
(left), and 157bl; Image #LS3-26: 177

Courtesy of the American Numismatic Society
52tr, 94tr, 142t

Art Resource
© V&A Images, London/ Art Resource, NY: 32; Jennifer Steele/
Art Resource, NY and © estate of Bargadubu, licensed by
Aboriginal Artists Agency Ltd.: 44

**© 2016 Artists Rights Society (ARS), New York/ VISCOPY,
Australia (Photo by Denis Finnin/AMNH)**
45

The Bridgeman Art Library
© Pictures from History/Bridgeman Images: 28–29cb, 100;
© Palazzo Sandi-Porto (Cipollato), Venice, Italy/Bridgeman
Images: 98–99; © The Trustees of the Chester Beatty Library,
Dublin: CBL C 1001, f. 10: 151r

© The British Library Board, I.O. ISLAMIC 966, f.63
159

Brooklyn Museum
Statuette of Nemesis in Form of Female Griffin with Wings, 2nd century C.E. Faience, Brooklyn Museum, Charles Edwin Wilbour Fund, 53.173. / Photo: © American Museum of Natural History / Denis Finnin : 54l

Courtesy of the Cavin-Morris Gallery NY
38br

Depositphotos
© homank76: 169b; Irmairma (l, r borders): 86–87; © Katja87: 57tr, © magicinfoto: 61b, © obencem: 66 (center), © ohmaymay: 152–53; © Stanislaw: 36-37; © vincenstthomas: 170

© Dorset Fine Arts (Photo by Denis Finnin/AMNH)
42b

Dover
Medieval_Design-0486998444 (l, r borders): 46–47, 140–43

Germanisches Nationalmuseum
77t

Digital images courtesy of the Getty's Open Content Program
ii; vi–vii (t, b borders), 55 (center), 73 (center), 97, 133, 164, 183

Getty Images
© De Agostini Picture Library/ Getty Images: 25b

The Granger Collection, New York
103 (right)

iStockphoto
© &#169 Matthias Straka: 180–81; © 9comeback: 119tr, 153t, 154t; © Aleksander Mirski: 157r; © AlexanderZam: 115tl; © ANGELGILD: 117; © boogieelephant: 69; © bülent gültek: 51tr, 55tr; © ChrisGorgio: 101, 182t; © daikokuebisu: viitr; 158l, 168t; © duncan1890: 13r, 38tl; © GomezDavid: 161b; © Helena Lovincic: 182cl; © icedea: 149, 157tl; © ilbusca: 81, 84t, 179r; © jcrosemann (l, r borders): 28–29, 60–61, 110tl, 123tr, 124–27, 160-61; © jirivondracek: 171; © mastapiece: 104tl; © Matt84: 20; © Nancy Nehring: 114bl; © NataliaBarashkova: 106; © Øystein Lund Andersen: 109r; © powerofforever: 26cr; © praditp: 113; © Sisoje: 115br; © skynavin: 112; © stockcam: 144b, 146-47; © VeraPetruk: 42tl; © wasja: 145tr; © Whiteway: 142b

Courtesy Internet Archive
https://archive.org/details/extinctbirdsatte00roth: 3
https://archive.org/details/brownfairybook00langrich: 24bl
https://archive.org/details/sightsinbostonsu1856midg2: 47b
https://archive.org/details/chamberssencyclo08phil: 72b
https://archive.org/details/UlyssisAldrovanIAldr: 136b, 176tl

Courtesy of the John Carter Brown Library at Brown University
145

© Frans Lanting / www.lanting.com
104br

Joe Leonard, Custom Woodcarving, Garrettsville, OH
Photo: © American Museum of Natural History /Denis Finnin: 53, 95

Courtesy Library of Congress
Prints and Photographs Division: LC-DIG-jpd-00628: xiii; LC-DIG-jpd-01559: 4; LC-USZ62-128102: 15b; LC-DIG-ppmsca-03955: 92b; Carol M. Highsmith, LC-DIG-highsm-11756: 94b; Alice S. Kandell, LC-DIG-ppmsca-30773: 110–11; LC-DIG-jpd-00323: 126; LC-USZC4-11627: 143l; LC-USZC4-11248: 143r; LC-USZC4-10363: 160c; LC-DIG-jpd-01469: 163b; LC-DIG-jpd-00088: 166; LC-DIG-jpd-01531: 167

Geography and Map Division: 22, 33, 134–35

The Mariners' Museum & Park, Newport News, VA
(Photo by Denis Finnin/AMNH): 34tl

Mary Evans Picture Library
© Mary Evans Picture Library: 104cl, 158br

Minden Pictures
© Norbert Wu/ Minden Pictures: 15t